AF140034

About this book

The book „Long live the…" combines a series of erotic short stories, which were written over a longer period of time. All stories in this collection illuminate a short excerpt from the life of one or more persons, which can only cover a few hours, but also one night, as well as a few days or nights.

Each short story is based on a theme that is illuminated by the author. People are characterized, places and scenes are described vividly. The short stories always develop from general events and are skilfully guided by the author to the erotic - sexual part of the story. This can be humorous to piquant, without ever slipping into the pornographic.

Long live the .... Love - Lust and Passion is a book for adults and is suitable for sweetening some relaxing hours for the reader.

The Author
After two novels by Xenia Marita Riebe have been published by B.Kühlen Verlag so far, she presents a series of erotic short stories for the first time in this book.
Her previous literary work ranges from writing short stories for magazines, magazines and anthologies, writing scripts and novels, co-founding and publishing a magazine for art and culture - DER OBSIDIAN - to running an internet blog - Blue Blog - on which she deals with art, literature and nature.

Xenia Marita Riebe worked as a visual artist for three decades and became famous with her sculptures made of newspaper. In this context, an art book about her Global Citizen ART project, of which she is the author, was also published.

Xenia Marita Riebe

Long live...
Love, Lust, Passion

Erotic Short Stories

2019

Translated into English by Bernd Riebe

Impressum

Blue Blog Edition

1. Edition 2019
Translated from the German
Es lebe die..Liebe, Lust, Leidenschaft
Text: © Xenia Marita Riebe
Cover design: © Xenia Marita Riebe
Drawings: © Xenia Marita Riebe
Layout: © Bernd Riebe
Printing and Publishing: BoD – Books on Demand, Norderstedt

ISBN 978-3-73862-409-0

Content

The Bet – Seduction in the Sauna Area

My friend Janine and I were sitting in a hotel bar. We had taken a few days off to recover from our exhausting job as stewardesses. Janine's relationship didn't run smoothly either and she was urgently looking for some distance to her long-time boyfriend. I didn't have to be considerate of anyone at that time, because my short but violent affair with a flight captain was just over. We drank Obstler, a schnapps that is very popular in the Bavarian Alps. Our wellness hotel was located in the snow-covered Allgäu.
We had spent the afternoon in the spacious sauna landscape of the hotel, because we both loved the relaxation that only an extensive sauna visit can bring about.
The fruit schnapps tasted very good. We drank it warm - at room temperature - and tried several varieties. I liked Williams Christ best and I just ordered the third glass when Janine started talking about the sauna.

"Do you remember the beautiful man with the little braid?" she asked and smiled dreamily into herself.
"You mean the one with the brown skin and the well-built body," I asked back. "Of course I remember. How could I not?
"He would be just the right person to forget Malte for a while," she thought.
"You would betray Malte?"
"No, I wouldn't betray him, of course. But I would like a little sex with this beautiful southerner. It's just such a fantasy."
"I think you're right," I said.
Normally I'm not into one-night stands and I only get involved with a man when I fall in love with him.
Nevertheless, I found that Janine was good for a little variety because she had been with Malte for far too long.
Janine looked at me in wonder with her dark eyes.
"You advise me to be unfaithful?
I just laughed and ordered another fruit brandy for both of us. We cheered each other up.
"Oh, the beautiful one had his young wife with him," Janine sighed.
"Yes, the one with the big round bottom," I giggled. The fruit schnapps already showed their effect.
"You know," I said evocatively. "Most women in the sauna weren't half as attractive as we were. They were all too fat, had sagging buttocks and unattractive breasts. And they were all boring. I bet that each of the men there would get involved in a quickie with you or me. And right there, right in front of their wives."

Janine laughed: "Well, you might have ideas! Do you think the women allow themselves to be deceived so easily by their husbands?

"They wouldn't even notice it', I said. "They are far too busy with themselves and most of them seem not to be interested in their husbands for a long time.

"That's true. Most couples seem to be completely indifferent to each other. The women read, the men doze off. That's terrible, isn't it?"

"It should be fun to lure the guys out of their reserves," I laughed.

"Oh, you are drunk. How do you want to do that?

"Look at me! Do I have a nice body or not?"

"Yes, you do! Without a doubt," Janine admitted.

"Your bottom is round and firm, but not too small, your breasts are wonderful and your skin is soft and firm.

"Oh, thank you. Too much of an honour.

"No, that simply corresponds to the facts', Janine laughed. "Your ethereal charisma and your beautiful blonde hair are added. Do you think I don't see all men turning around after you?

I laughed.

"Yes, if one manages to have a quickie with strange men in the sauna, then it is you," Janine laughed.

She really got going now. She seemed to like the thought of this adventure.

"I bet you can seduce ten men in one afternoon," she speculated.

Slowly I also began to warm up for the theme and I felt a slight tingling sensation in the pubic area. The fire in the open fireplace crackled and a pleasant warmth ran through my body. How nice it was to sit here with Janine and cook up crazy stories.

"Let's say eight', I returned. "What do you want to bet?

"Are you serious?" Janine asked and looked at me from big eyes.

"Why not. I am free and can do what I want. So, what do we bet on?

"I don't know." Janine seemed insecure.

"But I know," I replied. "If I can get eight men to stick it in me and do at least ten shots, then you must lure the Southerner into your bed.

"You really want to try it, don't you?

"Yes, tomorrow. That is something completely new. I've never experienced anything like it before, not even in my imagination.

"I think you'd better live it up there, too. If the story stands out - and it will - then we can pack our bags. And it's over with our nice stay here."

"Oh, don't be so afraid. Let me at least try it. When I realize it's too delicate, I can stop."

"And what do you do if you lose the bet?

"Well, then I'll seduce the beautiful southerner," I laughed. "But I will not lose. You will see! Are you going to hit it or not?"

The next day Janine went ahead to the sauna. Nobody should know that we are friends.

When I entered the sauna area, Janine was lying on a couch, wrapped in one of the white hotel bathrobes, pretending to read. Some guests were already present, all wrapped in the same white bathrobes or white sauna towels. I, on the other hand, wore my silk kimono. Pigeon blue with dainty pink blossoms it played around my figure in a very delicate way. I had put up my thick blond hair carelessly. I was excited, but didn't let it show. Lasciviously I took a seat on a couch and stretched my body comfortably. In addition I let a content sigh hear. I was sure that all the men present had noticed me with interest.

A few minutes later I watched a man about 40 years old leave his place. When he took off his bathing shoes and hung his towel on the hook in front of the Laconium - a sauna form from the south of Greece - I saw that he had quite a belly base. Hairy as he was, he wasn't exactly the type of man I liked. But if I wanted to win my bet, I couldn't be choosy! In addition the Laconium with its maximum temperature of 55° was a good place to make the first attempt. So as soon as the man had disappeared, I got up and followed him. His wife raised her eyes briefly, but seemed to see no competition in the slender young woman I was. She continued to read her thick novel calmly.

I took off my kimono and entered the laconium. The man had already settled on one of the curved stone benches, which were covered with small green mosaic stones. His sleeping penis lay relaxed between his thighs. My task now was to wake him up. And I lost no time.

I sat directly opposite him on a bench next to the fresh water fountain, which was actually used to raise ones legs. I looked the man straight in the eye and felt it confused him.

"I saw you here yesterday', I began timidly. "I like you', I added.

The man pointed with his index finger at himself and asked: 'I? You mean me?

"Yes, there is nobody else here, is there?"

He laughed tensely.

I got up and sat down behind the fountain to be protected from the outside view.

"Come,' I lured, stretched my foot into his field of vision and made a luring movement with it.

Nothing happened.

"We don't have much time and there isn't a second chance," I said more specifically. "So, what is it? Do you want me?

Now he had understood and when he came over to me, his penis wasn't sleeping anymore. I slipped onto the edge of the bench and he knelt before me on the folded towel I had laid on the tiled floor. Without hesitation, he penetrated me and began to push into me regularly as if it were a matter of course. Many a sigh slipped away from him and I had to calm him down with signs, because I was afraid they would hear us outside. I admit that the situation turned me on and I did not escape after the agreed ten shocks. I let him go and enjoyed sleeping with a complete stranger in a public sauna. He, too, seemed overwhelmed by the situation, for he soon had an orgasm. Afterwards he collapsed panting and sweating over me and lay on top of me for a short moment. Then he withdrew quickly and left the Laconium in a hurry. I heard him moaning loudly under the cold shower and had to smile. He would not forget this sauna so soon.

When I left the laconium shortly afterwards, I winked at Janine and showed her a hidden finger. I had already seduced a man. The first part of the bet was over.

I went to the showers, washed myself and cooled down. Then I strolled back to my couch. I needed a little time to choose a new candidate. I looked unobtrusively into the round. It was still quite early and so far only four men were to be seen. Two lay well-behaved next to their wives and kept their eyes closed, a lanky man with grey fuzzy hair just rose - he seemed to be alone - and my Laconium friend was running excitedly around outside. When he finally came back to his wife, he pretended that he had become dizzy in the sauna and lay still on his couch. The tall man had meanwhile walked through the outside area towards a door on which there was a word in ornate letters that I could not decipher from my couch. He opened the door and went through. I thought only briefly, then seized the opportunity and followed him. On the door behind which he had disappeared, I now saw that it said "Earth Sauna". I had never heard of one like it before. I imagined that the guests were lying there on benches on which topsoil was spread. But when I entered, I saw an anteroom with round shower cubicles and a door as if to a normal sauna. I opened it and slipped in. The man had laid down on the middle floor, and because of his height he had placed two sauna towels underneath. Now I saw that he was very slim and narrow and completely hairless. This made his penis look like that of a not yet sexually mature boy. He lay long and narrow on his master's right leg. The man had closed his eyes and did not look up when I entered. That made it difficult for me to flirt with him, for I could not address him so easily after all. I thought for a moment and then went straight on to attack. Why waste valuable time?

I squatted astride his hips and leaned my upper body down towards him. I looked at his face and when he opened his eyes in horror I noticed the particularly bright blue of his iris.

"What are you doing," he asked.

"What does it look like?' I whispered. "I thought we could pass the time here a little.

Then suddenly the thought came to me that the man could be gay.

"You like women, don't you?" I asked to be sure.

"Yes, I do.

I felt his penis straightening up under me.

"So, do you agree? With a quickie, I mean. Because I'm a little cool."

"It's only going to be a maximum of 55° here," he said.

I found this remark rather strange. Probably the situation made him embarrassed.

"Are you a prostitute?" he asked then.

"No. I'm a woman looking for a little sex."

With these words I reached for his penis, straightened it up and slid on it. The man moaned loudly and I put my hand lightly on his mouth.

Then I began to move on him. I counted the shocks and wanted to stop at the agreed ten, but only slipped off him at number 29. When he noticed this, he held me by the hips.

"What is going on, is something wrong?" he asked.
"Oh yes, all is well. I just think someone is coming. I heard the outer door.

And right, a few seconds later the door to the sauna was opened and a young couple came in. I pretended I was about to change my position, sat on my towel and stayed seated for a few minutes. The man was still lying on his back, as if nothing had happened. Only he had covered his penis with a corner of his towel. I smiled. The young people had to think he was pretty uptight. After a few minutes I left the earth sauna and took a shower in the anteroom.

Again on my couch I sent Janine a short message. "2 done," I wrote and added a laughing smilie. She nodded imperceptibly in my direction and sent me a raised thumb.

I rested a little. The afternoon was still long.

After a while, three men came in. A small round with a bald head, a stocky coaster with black curls and a big broad-shouldered one with a blond plait. The three of them immediately spread quite a bit of anxiety because they joked and laughed together. Immediately the reading women gave them reproachful looks.

In the meantime some women had also come to the

sauna. One just went to the Finnish sauna, another came from the steam sauna. It became clear to me that it would now be more difficult to seduce a man, because I had to expect to be disturbed at any moment. But what could have happened to me? I was alone here and - unlike my victims - had nothing to fear. So I sat like a spider in the web and waited for my next prey.

It didn't take long until the big one with the braid disappeared into the area with the different showers. I stood up and followed him. He stood under the light shower and seemed to shower himself with a comfortable temperature. I quickly hung my kimono on a hook and slipped under the water with him.

"Oops," he exclaimed and I noticed that he thought it was quite normal for a woman to approach him with a certain intention.

"Let's not lose any time," I said boldly, "Or don't you want to?"

And if he wanted to. He lifted me up and introduced his phallus into me. It was magical. The man had loosened his hair and he behaved like a stallion during sex. He threw his mane back and forth and splashed the water of the shower. The colorful light turned the splashes into shining drops and the finer ones into translucent prisms. The man came quickly and I slid down from him. I kissed him on the shoulder and disappeared in the shower opposite. My supposed victim tried to talk to me. But I remained mute and gave him a sign that I did not want more of him.

I left the shower and took a towel from the shelf to

dry my wet hair. They had come loose and hung with wet and heavy on their backs. Then I went to the Finnish sauna. Having sex there seemed to be a challenge to me. 90° Celsius are no small thing. Let's see, I thought if there is a man who follows me here. In the meantime, the men must have noticed which game I was playing. And in fact the small round ventured into the cave of the lioness.

He was embarrassed when he entered and remained undecided with the sauna towel in his hand.

"Did your friend tell you about me?" I helped him.

"Yes, he said that you were hot for sex.

"That's true. And you?

He pointed to his penis, which had already erected itself energetically.

"Have you ever done it at such a temperature?" I asked, fearing that he might die of a heart attack..

"No, but I sauna regularly and am used to the heat. I think I can take it."

"I'm coming down,' I said. "It's not so hot on the lower bench."

All gentleman, he spread out his towel invitingly. I crawled down and brought myself into the quadruped position. The man understood immediately and kneeled behind me. Seconds later he penetrated me and began to move slowly and carefully.

A connoisseur, I thought. He seemed to believe that we have eternal time. But he was wrong. I had just counted ten shocks when I saw a shadow at the door. I whispered: "Attention!

Then I quickly dropped on my stomach. The fat guy

immediately got up and climbed onto the middle bench. Then the door was opened and the third of my friends came in.

"Man, did you frighten me now, Ulli!" my disappointed partner gasped.

"Weren't you finished with the little one yet," Ulli asked suggestively. "Then I can go on for you.

I took him at his word and told him to lie on top of me. I spread my legs and whispered: "Well, then come and show me what you can do".

"But you can't do that!

"And if you can," Ulli replied. "You can watch." Already he lay on top of me and took me. Again I counted and was aware that the fat man was watching us. This was another attraction for me. Not only that I was already doing it that afternoon with the fifth stranger in a public sauna, no, a second man was watching me. I drifted on a wave of lust and allowed Ulli to stay in me far longer than planned. Together with him I had an orgasm and when he broke away from me I remained lying with my eyes closed. Suddenly I felt someone lying on top of me.

"Yes, that's right, Werner," Ulli cheered the small rounds on. "Give it to her. You weren't finished yet".

I didn't like that at all. I determined the rules of the game here. I wanted to push Werner away, but he was too heavy and couldn't be impressed. Ulli I heard slide over us.

"Show her" and "Keep it up", he cheered on his friend.

So I let it happen that also Werner satisfied himself

with me. The friends then left the sauna cabin together. Outside I heard them making big jokes and I asked myself for the first time whether I should break the bet. More than half the men were done. Would I be able to seduce three more?

The next opportunity offered itself to me when a man - he did not seem to be quite young any more, perhaps in his early sixties - went into the brine bath. I let a few minutes pass and followed him. The three friends made signs with a grin and I wondered if word had got around what I was doing here. I looked over at Janine asking questions, but she didn't move.
So I courageously opened the door. The man sat relaxed on a bench covered with small dark blue tiles. He didn't seem to suspect with what intention I was visiting him. He was a belly girder and his penis could hardly be seen underneath this rather mountainous area. It didn't make much sense to sit on him. So I kneeled down on the bench opposite him and stretched out my butt towards him. The man didn't react. I wiggled back and forth a little and then asked over my shoulder, "Do you feel like having some sex?
"What?" the man asked.
"You understood correctly. You may, if you want.
"But..."
"If you hesitate much longer, the chance is over," I urged. "No one can see us from outside. The window is all misted up".
Then he got up and stood behind me. It took him a while, but then I felt him inside me. This time I was

determined to really put an end to it after ten pushes, but then the man touched me so much in his awkwardness that I let him go a little.

Finally I said: "Enough for today! Enough is enough Frightened, the man withdrew and I left the brine bath as quickly as possible.

In the meantime it had become dark outside. I needed some fresh air and went outside. There were loungers to rest on. I lay on my back, covered myself with a blanket and looked up at the stars. So I lay about ten minutes when Janine sat down on the couch next to mine.

"Well, haven't you had enough?" she asked.

"Yes, I did. But now I have already managed six, I cannot give up there.

"You are unbelievable', Janine said admiringly. "I would never have believed that you would dare that. Then the door opened and a man came out. Janine rose and, demonstrating indifference, went into the anteroom to the earth sauna. The man lay down on one of the loungers. His body steamed. He must have just come out of the Finnish sauna. I gave him a few minutes before I started my attack. The outside area was of course a dangerous place because it was only separated from the sauna area by high glass doors. In daylight the sauna guests could see and follow every movement in the outdoor area from inside. Now, of course, it was dark and only two candles were lit outside. The interior, on the other hand, was brightly lit. This made the view from inside to outside more difficult. Now it was rather like that that one could look at the sauna guests from the outside as watching fish in an aquarium.

I straightened up and let my towel slide slowly to the floor. I saw the man watching me from the corner of his eye, like many men do in the sauna. They pretend to sleep, but secretly look after every naked woman. I shamelessly took advantage of this by slowly letting my silk kimono glide over my shoulders first and then over my naked breasts. When it had slipped to the waist, I stood up, pulled it out and laid it on the couch. On the outside there was a kind of platform made of dark wood, the sense and purpose of which was not quite clear to me. The platform was a little behind and in relative darkness. It had a canopy supported by two thick round wooden columns. Three steps led up to the platform, which was barren and empty in the cold mountain air. The platform was bordered by a wall. I climbed the steps and looked smiling over my shoulder.

The man looked at me with interest. What might he think?

I leaned with my back against the smooth wooden column and gave a sigh. I listened, but nothing moved. The man did not seem to understand. There I pushed my bottom a little to the back out and moved it, so that it became visible times on the left and times on the right of the column. But in vain I waited for a reaction. Finally I turned lasciviously around and embraced the column with the left arm. So I could stretch my upper body forward and show the man my breasts. I smiled at him and lured him with my finger. He turned as if to see if someone was standing behind him. But there was nobody to whom my curls could have been directed.

"Do you mean me?" he asked in surprise.

I just nodded and threw him a kissing hand. Then he understood and rose from the couch. When he threw off the blanket, I saw his unsightly body. He was soft and fat, had women's breasts, a hanging belly and X-legs.

Why were there so few handsome men here!

With a horny facial expression the man now came up the stairs to me and stood behind me. His hands embraced my breasts and kneaded it around. I closed my eyes and imagined that the beautiful one with the dark hair Janine was supposed to seduce was standing behind me.

The stranger now gasped quite violently at my left ear and I told him not to take back any longer. Then he pulled my hips back with his hands, so that my bottom came towards him and shortly afterwards he penetrated me from behind.

Again I counted, because I wanted to get rid of the unaesthetic man as quickly as possible. But ten shocks are simply over too quickly and it is too difficult to break off the sex after such a short time. So I let him have it longer than I wanted. He pushed violently into me and moaned quite loudly. I didn't stop him because I was sure no one out here would hear him. Suddenly the door to the outside area was opened and a woman stuck her head outside.

"Horst, are you here?" she asked and looked over at the couches.

The man paused and I felt his penis shrinking inside me. Needless to say, he closed my mouth. The woman had barely closed the door when he withdrew from me.

"My wife", he said with panic in his voice. "She is looking for me.

And already he stumbled down the stairs and disappeared in the anteroom to the earth sauna.

I shivered and also went through the door with the ornate letters. I winked conspiratorially at the man standing under the warm shower and went into the sauna cabin. There I met Janine.

"That was number seven," I said. "Behind the column on the pedestal. He almost got caught by his wife. Just went well again."

Then we heard a woman's voice outside: "Horst, here you are! I looked everywhere for you!

"I was cold and I went into the earth sauna for a moment," Horst lied.

Janine and I crawled giggling into the back corner of the sauna to hide from the woman who would otherwise have been able to see us through the small window in the sauna door. Only when the couple had left the anteroom did we laugh.

"If she knew what her Horst was doing here," Janine laughed.

"Yes, but she would not believe him, even if he freely confessed.

Now that I was slowly getting hungry, I wanted to get the last quickie behind me as quickly as possible. My eyes fell on a young couple who had probably entered the sauna area while I was outside busy with Horst. It sat on the foot basin in the middle of the room. The young woman was quite pretty and had a good figure, the young man was beautiful and handsome. But the two did not seem to have to say themselves much and bored themselves completely obviously.

This should be my last challenge, I thought. But how can I lure him away from her? Then chance came to my aid.

"I forgot my day care in the room," I heard the young woman say. "I'll go upstairs and get her."

The beauty remained alone. Now I only had to address him. I strolled towards him and whispered in passing: "Will you come to the steam sauna with me? I want to show you something.

I touched his chest slightly with my fingertips. He drove together as if electrified and looked up at me. What he saw seemed to please him, for he gave me a radiant smile.

I knew he had taken the bait!

So I walked slowly and with swaying hips over to the steam sauna. I opened the door and disappeared into the dense steam. Here you could not be seen from outside and even inside you could hardly see your own hand in front of your eyes. I spread out my towel on the bright stone bench and lay down with my thighs spread so that he would have the right view if he followed me. And in fact I didn't have to wait long.

The door was opened and there he stood. In the same second his penis swelled to a stately size.

"Is that what you wanted to show me," he asked.

"Yes, do you like it? Then come. It belongs to you for a short time.

He didn't want to be told twice. With youthful verve he came over to me, placed his hands next to my shoulders and supported his upper body up. He looked directly at me.

"Who are you," he wanted to know.

"That doesn't matter. Take me, or go!

He looked at me skeptically for a moment, as if he was smelling a nasty trap. But then he lost his suspicion and took the opportunity for a short adventure. He penetrated me and began to move mechanically. I immediately noticed that he was an unimaginative lover. What a pity! He was the first man that afternoon whose looks I liked, but during sex he was really boring. That's why I pushed him away soon and asked him to leave. When he retired, he looked at me in disbelief.

"That was it??" he asked.

"Looks that way', I gave back. "Chance not used - opportunity over!

I took my towel and pushed myself past him to the exit. Then he grabbed my arm and tried to hold me back.

"Your wife just came back," I said. "You don't want her to notice anything, do you?

He let me go immediately. I slipped out of the steam sauna and went into the shower area to take a good

shower.
I had won the bet!

In the evening at the bar I told Janine in detail about my experiences and we had a great time.
"But you already know that it's your turn now," I asked and gave her a slight elbow thrust. Tomorrow I want to see how you seduce the beautiful southerner.
Janine blushed.
"Let's see," she said.
"You must! You have lost the bet,' I outraged myself.
"Admit it,' Janine replied. "It was fun for you to prove your seduction skills. Would you do it again?"
"Yes, it was exciting, I admitted. "But no, I wouldn't do it again. It was an experience and that's enough."
I looked at Janine thoughtfully.
"I now know that I am suitable as a prostitute," I laughed. "But I'd rather stay a stewardess!

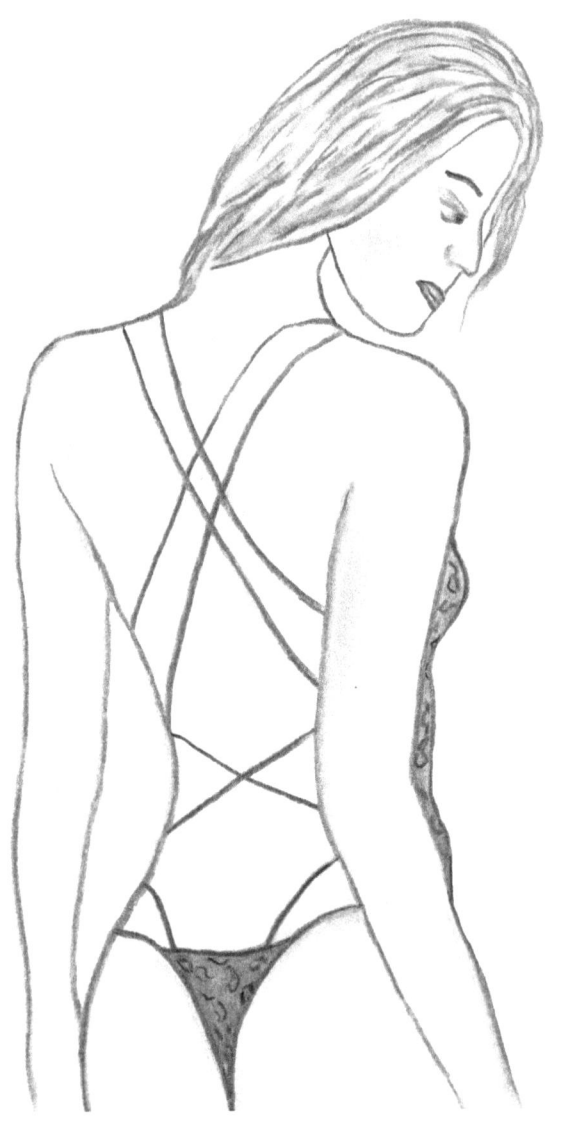

Test Lying in the bed store

There is a small Danish town called Egå which is situated on the west coast of Denmark. There is a warehouse in an industrial estate, whose gates have been replaced by modern automatic glass doors. A large sign outside the hall announces what is inside. "Bettenlager" (bed store) stands there in large white letters on a red background.
Inside the building, one bed stands next to the other, all fitted with mattresses with protective covers. On the walls of the hall there are various slatted frames in specially designed holders. Next to them there are upright mattresses in all strengths and designs.
Beds and mattresses are the core business of Björn Anderson's bed store. The young man recently started his own business here. Björn also sells duvets and bed linen and various small items of furniture such as

bedside cabinets and chests of drawers. But because he's new to the business, he thought long and hard about how to lure people into his shop.

To set himself apart from big furniture stores like the Swedish IKEA, Björn tried to focus entirely on customer service. He advertised on the internet, in newspapers and on billboards as follows: "Come to the bed store in Egå. Here you will be given personal advice and you will be able to try it out as often and as long as you like".

Little by little the first customers came to the store, mostly couples who were really looking for a bed or a mattress and sometimes even bought one. But sales were sluggish. In order to boost this, Björn had the idea of looking for a pretty Danish girl who would smile from his advertisements and posters. He looked around the job exchange and found Smilla, a very pretty blonde with a good figure. Slim and busty, she was the ideal figurehead for a bed store.

At the photo shoot Smilla acted very skilfully, let the photographer direct her into different poses on the prepared bed and showed a radiant smile. She was lightly dressed, wearing a satin negligee with spaghetti straps in a warm mocha tone. Smilla was so likeable and uncomplicated with the photos that Björn felt the need to always have her around.

After the shootin was finished, he asked her to his office at the end of the hall. He paid her for her services and asked her if she had a permanent job. She hadn't and when he offered her a job as a saleswoman in his bed store, he got to know Smilla's ambition for

32

the first time.

"You know," Smilla said and smiled charmingly. "Shop assistant is not the right thing for me. I've set myself the goal of earning a lot of money and that's why such a job is out of the question for me."

"Too bad," Björn replied disappointedly. "I am sure that a number of men would come here to buy a bed if they knew that you would advise them.

"Then make me your partner," Smilla returned, "and I promise you the business will go well. You would also profit from that.

Björn looked at her in amazement.

"Well, you're really going for it," he said.

"I know my price', she smiled, 'I am still young and beautiful and I have to take advantage of that. You know, I didn't really learn anything. I didn't feel like staying long with an apprenticeship and then doing a boring job and earning just enough to just survive. That's not my thing. I want more from life and I will get it. If not here, then somewhere else."

Björn thought about it. What could happen if he made Smilla a partner? But he had to take his time to think about it.

"I have your telephone number', he remarked and said goodbye to her.

But he couldn't get Smilla out of his head. He almost always thought of her. Her enchanting smile, her beautiful breasts that had looked so boldly from the neckline of the negligee, her round bottom over the smooth long legs. Smilla had enchanted him and so he threw all his doubts overboard and made her his partner.

On Smilla's first working day, Björn tried to work with her on a concept that would help her attract customers to the bed store. But Smilla already had a plan that she openly presented to him.
"We have to rely on my sex appeal," she explained, "Word must get around that men here are being served by a provocative woman. Every customer who has been here has to brag about it to his friends, you know?
"And what are you going to do??"
"Just let me do it. We want to increase sales and that only requires a little skill in dealing with customers. You take care of the office stuff. I'll take care of the sales."
Björn was beaten. He had nothing against Smilla's unyielding will.
"But you're not doing dirty work here," he warned her.
"No, of course not. What do you think?" Smilla returned laughing.

The first customer entered the bed store. Smilla walked towards him with a friendly smile. She wore a very tight, very short red skirt and a semi-transparent black blouse.
"Can I help you," she asked and showed her most beautiful smile.
"I'm looking for a mattress," said the customer.
On the way to the mattresses, Smilla looked at the

customer from the corner of her eye. He was tall, redheaded and had freckles and did not look bad overall.

Smilla explained the advantages of the individual mattresses to him and then invited him to lie down and try them out. The customer followed her to the beds.

"Please lie down here," Smilla asked the customer. "By the way, I am Smilla. And what is your name?

"Lars", the customer said wondering at her question.

"Ah, Lars," said Smilla. "A beautiful name. And how are you lying here, Lars?

Smilla sat down on the edge of the bed and looked at the customer. When she noticed that he was getting nervous, she quickly got up again. She didn't want to frighten him. She knew that you have to be careful with some men.

She led Lars to the next bed and shook up a feather pillow and put it under his head.

"Is this mattress right for you," Smilla asked. "Or is it too soft? Do you sleep alone at home or with a partner?

When the customer didn't answer, she knew he was single. This increased the sales prospects.

She then took his hand and lured him from bed to bed.

When he was lying on a French bed, Smilla lay down spontaneously next to him and pretended to demonstrate how to use a side sleeper pillow. Her hand touched his loins only very briefly and as if by chance.

Lars blushed.

"I think you should take this bed here," said Smilla, in order to cover the embarrassing situation for him. She stood up and looked at the price tag. "The bed here with the mattress is only slightly more expensive than the single mattress over there. And it suits you. You are a French type. That's why you should sleep in a French bed. And there's room for a girlfriend here too."

When Lars left the bed, he had actually bought the bed. Confused, but very excited, he left the industrial estate with the paid bill.

In the evening at the gym he told a group of men about the sexy waitress in the bed store and about the fact that she had grabbed his penis. There was a certain excitement in the men's group and they wanted to know where this bed store was.

"You probably all need a new bed, too," laughed Lars, happy that his story had gone down so well.

The next day a pretty good-looking blond came to the bed camp.

"I heard from an acquaintance that they give excellent advice here," he said when Smilla greeted him.

"I'm glad to hear that," Smilla returned. "What can I do for you?

She asked this question in a deliberately offensive tone and felt that the customer was on fire immediately.

"A bed," he returned, and his voice did not sound so self-confident anymore.

Smilla led him straight to the test lying and since the customer had apparently already heard from her, she did not proceed as cautiously as she had done with Lars. She asked for his first name and right next to the first bed she lay down next to him and looked at him provocatively.

Ole, the customer's name, looked straight into her eyes. The bed didn't seem to interest him any more. But Smilla praised the advantages of the bed without letting go of his gaze. Then she put her hand on his chest and nestled her head to his shoulder.

"You see,' she said.

Now Ole sensed his chance, took Smilla's hand and pressed it onto his penis.

"Well, how do you like that," he asked. "Can I pick you up after work?"

"I can't leave until I've sold enough. My boss is strict. So what is it, are you buying the bed? Then I'll finish early."

Ole bought the bed, the mattress and bed linen as well.

"I'll pick you up tonight," he said when he left the bed. Smilla laughed and had her thoughts about it.

Björn was highly satisfied with the sales results achieved by his partner. Smilla sold one bed after the other and mostly enough accessories. Her concept seemed to work, but it was also very hard on her. In the evening she disappeared through the back door, quickly got into her car and drove off on a side street. Björn was amused by the men who stood stealthily in front of the bed camp or waited in their cars. When he then closed the doors and drove home, he saw that the disappointed customers also made off. But Smilla hadn't promised either of them anything, she was just smart enough not to argue when a customer suggested picking her up. Once he had bought a bed, she was no longer interested in him.

But one day a man entered the bed store, and Smilla was immediately captivated. He was tall, sporty and a dark guy. He wasn't Danish, that was obvious. Danish men often tend to be soft and spongy. But this one was muscular, you could see that, and he had a smooth gait. The customer strolled between the beds and took a closer look at one or the other. Smilla watched him and she knew he was waiting for the erotic saleswoman he had heard about. She opened another button of her blouse and let a good part of her bosom see. Then she straightened her tight skirt and walked calmly towards the handsome man. As she approached, she noticed that he was wearing a groomed 3-day beard.

When he saw her, he smiled broadly and exposed even white teeth. Smilla was impressed, but didn't let it show.

"What can I do for you," she asked.

"Oh, I can think of quite a few things," the man replied.

Smilla felt that she blushed slightly. That had never happened to her before. She had to pull herself together and not allow the customer to take over at the helm completely.

"A mattress, I suppose," she said, trying to look calm.
"You need a new mattress or a bed.

"Right guess," said the man. "We're in a bed store."
He made a sweeping movement with his arms that
enclosed the whole room.

Smilla had to smile, but caught on quickly.

"We also sell other things," she returned.

"But I can't be test lying with them," said the
customer.

"What's your name," Smilla went on the offensive.

"Olaf, Johan, Aksel," the man returned. "Pick a name."
Smilla did not let herself be put off: "I like Johan", she
said, "and my name is Smilla".

"Beautiful name. Are you the one with the feeling for
snow?

Smilla smiled crookedly. "My intuition is directed
towards other things.

"I have already heard that. Your reputation precedes
you.

Smilla ignored this remark and said: "Well, then come
with me, Johan. I'll show you our latest models."

With a bold hip swing she walked towards a double
bed. But her otherwise unshakeable safety had begun
to waver.

She explained the advantages of the bed to Johan and
offered him a test bed. She put a protective foil on the
lower part of the mattress.

"You can keep your shoes on," she said. "Please," she
made an inviting gesture.

But Johan did not lie down on the bed. He stopped in

front of Smilla and looked challenging into her eyes. "What is it," she asked. "Don't you like the bed? Are you looking for a single bed or a French one?

Johan gave no answer. He just stood there and looked at Smilla openly.

After a few moments he said: "It is not the bed. I like wide beds with lots of room. But I don't like the timing."

"How should I understand that?

"You understand. It would suit me better if I could try the beds after closing time with you alone.

"That's impossible," Smilla replied, even though she felt her own heart beating up to her neck.

"Why? Don't you have a key to the hall?

"I do, that's not the problem."

"Yes, and then what hinders you?

Smilla thought for a moment.

"Tonight at nine. Back door," she said after a few moments, turned on the heel and walked away.

When Smilla entered the office, Björn looked up from a pile of bills.

"Is something wrong?" he asked.

"No, all was well. There was just one stupid customer, but he's gone again."

Smilla poured herself a cup of coffee and sat down at her workplace.

"Smilla", said Björn. "You have the blouse open. Did the guy touch you?"

"He tried, but I can defend myself. Don't worry."

"Actually, I don't like what you're doing out there with the customers, even though it's very good for sales.

You are much too good for such things, intelligent as you are."

Thank you," said Smilla, "but she didn't pay much attention to what Björn said.

Smilla had known for some time that Björn was in love with her. He had confessed to her and made it clear to her that he was not averse to a marriage with her.

"Then everything stays in the family," Björn had argued. "The business and the capital. That would be better for both of us.

But a marriage was not what Smilla wanted. She wanted to be rich and free and decide for herself how she wanted to shape her future life. And besides, she didn't like Björn. He was kind and friendly, but unattractive. Just a Dane. There was that man from just now something completely different. Exciting, mysterious and handsome. A real man, a doer, an alpha animal. Smilla surprised herself how much she had been impressed by Johan. What had this man done that she had almost lost control? Normally she always determined the rules of the game. And never before had she gone beyond a few erotic hints.

"Smilla," she heard Björn again, "are we going to have dinner tonight?

"I'm sorry, I can't. I have an appointment with a friend. But tomorrow I am free."

So I am determined to meet Johan tonight, she said in astonishment. It is already clear to me that this is not harmless. I don't even know the man. And with him alone in a large store full of beds in a lonely industrial area.

"You shouldn't do that, Smilla," she warned herself.
What if he doesn't come alone? She asked herself. If
he brings his buddies with him and they rape me? No,
Smilla, you cannot come here. Impossible! And yet she
knew that she would be there at nine o'clock in the
evening.

Smilla was wearing her normal everyday clothes when
she came back to the warehouse in her small car in the
evening. Jeans and T-shirt, a light jacket and boots
with moderately high heels. She looked like a normal
Danish girl. With the clothes of the day she had also
discarded her erotic charisma. In no way did she want
to irritate Johan into something she would not be able
to cope with. She parked her car away from the back
entrance and kept a close eye on the parking lot,
because she wanted to be sure that Johan was alone.
Otherwise she didn't want to leave her car. Until 9 pm
it was still a quarter of an hour. Smilla was nervous.
She still wondered why Johann magically captivated
her. He was not the first beautiful man she had met.
And yet he had something very special, something that
made her restless and careless.

While she was still brooding, a large black limousine,
an expensive Volvo, arrived. The driver of the car was
Johan. So he had actually come and he seemed to be
alone. Now he got out, locked the car and went to the
back door and knocked. Smilla gave herself a jolt and
left her car. She quickly went over to Johan, who
looked astonished when he saw her.

"What a transformation," he exclaimed. "From vamp to Cinderella."

Smilla blushed.

"I'm off work," she said, "and I'll dress as I please. Business is business, but we are here privately now, aren't we?

"Yes, yes, of course," Johan assured her.

Smilla unlocked the warehouse and they entered the office through which she led him to the salesroom.

"Sit down," she asked Johan. "I chilled a bottle of champagne for us. I'll be right there.

A little later she appeared with a tray of two glasses of sparkling wine on it. She raised her glass to him and they sat down on the large double bed. But Johan soon took the glass out of Smilla's hand and placed it on the bedside table. Then he bent over and kissed her long and passionately.

"You know what I came for," he said. "I want to sleep with you and as soon as possible.

Smilla became a little dizzy. Never before had she experienced a man who acted with such haste and determination and bluntly as Johan. But Johan gave her no time to think. In the twinkling of an eye he had taken off her T-shirt and jeans and nestelte at her bra fastener. When he took it off, he clicked his tongue. Smilla's breasts were beautiful and exactly the right size to be sexy and provocative.

"How beautiful you are," Johan said admiringly. "Let's see if the rest is so pretty."

And already he stripped off her panties. Now she lay completely naked on the bed, while Johann was still wearing his elegant suit.

He must be rich, it went through Smilla's head. The expensive car, the tailor-made suit, the elegant shoes made of the best leather. Maybe this is where my future lies.

"What are you thinking about," Johan asked. "You look so dreamy.

"Oh, nothing," she gave back and knelt before Johan to undo his tie.

She took off his white shirt and opened his belt.

"The shoes," he said as she tried to slip his pants down.

Smilla jumped off the bed and knelt down on the rug in front of Johan. While she opened his shoelaces and took off his shoes, she looked up at him in ecstasy.

Johan's chest was wide, his skin had a deep brown tone and he was slightly hairy.

"Where are you from," she asked.

"I was born in Copenhagen. Why do you ask?

"You are not a Dane," she said.

"Yes, I am Danish."

"But not native."

"My father was a Moorish sailor. But I never met him. When I was born, he was at sea again long ago and he never came back."

"Did he die at sea?" Smilla wanted to know.

"No, rather run away," Johan laughed.

Now Smilla took off his pants and boxer shorts and a magnificent erect penis appeared. He flinched darkly and eerily in his full size. Following an impulse, Smilla leaned forward and took the stranger in her mouth.

She did her job well, letting her lips and tongue play and got Johan excited to reach into her long blonde hair and bend her head back a little so he could see some of her mouth's play. Johan moaned loudly and violently and Smilla was worried that he might come in her mouth. So she unexpectedly released his penis and crawled onto Johan's bed. In the meantime he was so excited that he immediately penetrated her, lifted her legs to his shoulders and pushed her violently. Smilla tried to slow him down a little because she didn't want him to climax too quickly. But she didn't succeed. Johan behaved like a bull and soon came loud and violent. But he recovered quickly. He had cuddled up to Smilla's back and nibbled on her ear as she felt his penis swelling again.

"Keep it that way," he whispered into her ear and penetrated her in the classic spoon position.

Now he was a tender and attentive lover, taking care of Smilla's clitoris with his fingers and passionately kneading her breasts. Together they reached their climax.

Later, when they drank another glass of champagne, Johan asked: "Can we come back here tomorrow night?

Smilla thought about it. She didn't want to make it so easy for him. She also wanted to learn more about him and suggested going to a restaurant together.

"What for," Johan asked. "I don't want to eat with you, I want to have sex with you.

Although his impudence hurt Smilla, she was also impressed by his honesty.

"Well, what is it?", Johan urged. "Did you not like it? Oh, yes, Smilla thought and agreed to meet Johan again the following evening.

Smilla had just reached home when Johan called her. She was happy, because that meant that Johan had caught fire. He chatted a little with her, complimented her and said he was already longing for her back. Then his tone became more businesslike.

"Smilla, I want to suggest something to you," he said.

"Yes?"

She was alarmed. It would have been too nice if a man like Johan had fallen in love with her. Had he not called her Cinderella? And wasn't she also a Cinderella, beautiful, but poor?

"I have a business partner there', Johan began again.

"The man is already older and has a special fondness.

"And that would be?

"Well, how shall I put it? He likes to watch others have sex. And he pays well for it".

Smilla was so disappointed that her tears came to her eyes, but she didn't let on.

"You mean you want to bring him with you tomorrow. Then you want to sleep with me and he should watch us do it?

"Yes, that's how I thought it.

"I am not a prostitute," Smilla said angrily.

"You shouldn't sleep with him either. We will have it just as nice as today, only that he will sit quietly in an armchair and watch us. You will have forgotten him in a few minutes. He is very discreet."

46

"How much does he pay", Smilla asked in a businesslike tone.

"I knew you were a clever girl," Johan triumphed. "He pays 30,000 crowns. That is a lot of money.

Smilla swallowed. That was really a lot of money and it would bring her one step closer to her goal.

"I have to think about it," she said. "Call me again later."

She ended the conversation without saying goodbye and first took a Martini.

"Do you have any more business partners like that?" she asked when Johan called again later.

"Yes, some more. And they all pay well. Have you changed your mind?

"When do you want to come?

"At nine, like yesterday? Is that all right?"

Smilla drove her car towards the industrial estate. She felt queasy, but she was also excited. What she was about to experience had never occurred to her before. What would it be like if someone watched her have sex?

The dark Volvo drove up at the appointed time. Again Smilla sat in her small car and watched Johan and the stranger get out. She left her car and went over to the two men. She greeted them businesslike, unlocked the door and let the two men in. She had decided not to show emotion or feel anything. She just wanted to get the sex over with as quickly as possible. The joy of sleeping with Johan had passed her by. And yet she felt again the strong attraction that emanated from him.

The other man, who introduced himself as Carl, was old and had thick snow-white hair. He too was elegantly dressed and wore an expensive suit like Johan. He seemed likeable and friendly.

"Let's settle the business right here," Smilla suggested. It was easier for her to collect the money in the office than in bed. She then felt less like a whore.

"Of course," Carl said and handed her an envelope. Smilla took the banknotes from him and counted them. Then she locked the money in the desk drawer.

"Come with me," she said and led the men into the store room.

During the day, under the pretext of a new decoration, Smilla had pushed an armchair close to a French bed. Now she turned it so that Carl could sit in it and let his gaze glide freely over the bed.

Then she turned on a floor lamp and dimmed the ceiling light considerably. Finally she offered the voyeur a glass of sparkling wine, which Carl thankfully accepted.

As Smilla undressed, she felt the old man's gaze on her. And although Johan and Carl talked quietly, she knew the men wouldn't let her out of their sight.

When she was finally naked, she lay down on the bed and waited for the things to come. Then Johan pulled something out of his jacket pocket.

"Here put this on," he said and threw a bra and thong on the bed. "Carl likes it better when you have something on.

The lingerie was red and made of wafer-thin lace. Smilla smelled it briefly and then put it on. It fitted.

Apparently Johan had measured well the evening before.

Now Johan undressed and came to her on the bed. All romance between them had vanished. Johan conducted her so into the doggy position that she squatted sideways to her spectator. Then he pushed the thong a little to the side and penetrated her. Smilla looked stealthily past her thighs over to Carl. He had leaned forward so that he could see exactly how Johan took her. Smilla looked away. She wanted to forget Carl. At that moment Johan grabbed her thighs and put them around his waist and forced Smilla into a prone position. He had now taken control of her and after just a few minutes brought her into another position with strong grips. Again and again Smilla looked over to Carl. He sat tense but outwardly calm in his armchair. And suddenly Smilla felt a very peculiar tickle, which was probably due to the fact that she had sex in front of a spectator. She felt how the excitement gripped her and carried her away. She suddenly heard herself moaning, although she wanted everything to be cool and businesslike. But that was over now. She actively participated in the sex and met Johan demandingly with her bottom. He seemed happy about it because he smiled at her.

"You're great, girl', he whispered. "That makes it much more fun.

And in fact she finally forgot that an old horny man was watching. She didn't notice anymore that Carl was following her every move and that he was trying to memorize everything he saw.

But finally Johan was unstoppable and came inside her. He withdrew and left the bed to go to the toilet. Smilla was frightened. What did that mean? Did Johan deliberately leave her alone with Carl?

"Thank you," she heard Carl's polite voice. "You were a lot of fun to me. Can I give you an extra bonus?" He handed Smilla a few bills and when she accepted them, she felt like a whore for the first time. She swallowed, but soon regained her composure. She thanked and quickly dressed. When Johan came back naked, he looked at her in wonder.

"Already dressed? Maybe Carl wants to see more. But Carl beckoned away.

"It's enough for today," he said and Smilla was grateful to him. "But I will gladly come back.

From that day on Johan came to the bed store again and again in the evening with business friends. Sometimes it was a man who wanted to watch sex, sometimes it was two or three. They were always well-groomed gentlemen who were well-off. That made Smilla's job easier. If several men came she earned very well, since everyone had to pay for watching. Nevertheless she did not like to have sex in front of several spectators. The men, who had always known each other, talked and often commented on what they saw. They made each other aware when Smilla was having fun with sex and even went so far as to cheer Johan on to take her harder. But sometimes it also excited her when she became aware of the presence of the voyeurs.

But she liked the quiet old people much better, because they could at least forget her for a while. Smilla had gone over to undressing in the toilet and appearing at each bed in a slightly transparent black dressing gown, the edges of which were decorated with marabou feathers. Below it she usually wore a tangabody with crossed ribbons in her back. This seemed very erotic and had the advantage that she didn't have to undress in front of the men.

Smilla had already saved a nice sum of money when Björn came to the store one evening. He had forgotten something and wondered about the light coming out of the hall. He went in to put it out and found Smilla squatting on Johan and moving up and down on his penis while two guys watched.

When Smilla noticed Björn, she turned white and red alternately.

Björn turned around and left the bed store hastily.

"Björn, wait," Smilla shouted after him. "I can explain everything to you!

But then the door of the office slammed shut and the engine of Björn's car roared.

Horrified by the discovery and worried how Björn would take it, Smilla stopped having sex and asked the men to leave. On the way home, she kept thinking about how disappointed Björn must be of her. And he was right about that, too. She pondered how she could explain her behaviour to him. But was there even an explanation for what she had done?

For the first time in weeks she thought about it herself. Was it just the money that had irritated her?

Or was there more to it? She had to admit that she sometimes enjoyed sex with strangers. But often she didn't feel anything at all and only thought of all the money easily earned. She had often thought about stopping soon, but she had put it off again and again. And now it was too late. Björn would never forgive her.

And Smilla was right about that. Björn could not accept all the explanations she tried the next day. Deeply disappointed by her, he finally cancelled the partnership agreement and Smilla's time in the bed store in Egå ended.

The three Graces

Antonius Süßmundt is a passionate painter.
For years he has dedicated himself to the beautiful
sex. Canvases of all sizes pile up in his studio. And
they all show female nudes. Sensually depicted
beautiful bodies in sublime colors, whose curves are
emphasized by skilfully applied light and shadow
techniques. The observer looks at the paintings with
the devotion with which the painter guides the brush
when he brings round buttocks and well-formed
breasts onto the canvas. Each brush stroke is skillfully
placed and the ductus is fine and homogeneous.
Antonius has a special fondness for opulent women
with a slight belly build-up, and he attaches great
importance to the fact that the slight curvature above
the shame attracts the gaze. The artist hates painting
from photographs and so, whenever he has earned
enough money, he buys one or more models.

He has just lit the small iron stove in his studio. He is

expecting three young women to pose for a version of the "Three Graces". Antonius wants his models to feel comfortable so that they can relax. This is important for his work and he is willing to heat his studio. If he is alone, he often works in an unheated room, because wood is expensive and Antonius is poor. In winter he wears a thick padded jacket over his work shirt and fingerless gloves on his hands. A bold beret sits on his dark curls.

Antonius Süßmundt is a beautiful man. According to his appearance he could be Italian or French or a mixture of both. His eyes are coal-black and get a deep shine at work, his curved nose is big but not dominating and his mouth, with its beautifully curved lips, seems sensual and yet masculine. He is medium sized and slender. His movements are smooth and well set.

The sun is just sending his first rays through the west window of the studio when the doorbell rings. Antonius checks his props once more and then hurries to the door to open his models with the buzzer. Chattering and laughing, he hears them climb up the stairs. The women know each other, two of them are even close friends. All of them have already been his models.

The studio door is opened and the young women come in. They are wrapped in thick winter clothes and wear caps and scarves.

There is beautiful Anna, who now takes off her cap and releases a gush of red hair into freedom. Her tender, almost transparent skin, which is typical for women with natural red hair, is a little irritated by the cold.

Dora, a luxuriant blonde, laughingly puts her coat of fake fur on the chair and begins to take off her high boots. Her light blue eyes shine. She is a striking beauty who always seems to be in the best of moods.

"I hope it's warm enough," says Antonius and rubs her hands. "I turned on the stove two hours ago and have been heating up ever since."

"At the moment it feels nice and warm," Lisa replies. "We also come from the freezing cold. The east blows really hard today and cuts into the skin. Look how red my cheeks are."

"I made mulled wine," laughs Antonius. "I think we'll toast first. That warms and relaxes the mood. Well, what do you mean?

Shortly afterwards, they sit on the few pieces of furniture in the studio, each holding a cup of hot mulled wine in their hands. Lisa is still dressed in her yellow, soft wool sweater, which is too big for her and which with its oversized turtleneck accentuates her sensuality. Her shiny brunette hair and the brown deer eyes are set in scene by the warm yellow colour particularly beautifully.

Antonius sees this and plans to paint Lisa once in this sweater, under which her beautiful round butt and long slender legs are to be seen. Lisa is the most tender of the three women, her limbs are long and slender and her breasts a little too small for Antonio's taste. Nevertheless, he often asks her to be his model, for there is a very special expression in her brown eyes. He hasn't seen anything like it in any other woman. It lies between sensual and bold, between encouraging and thoughtful. He never knows where he is with her and this mystery in her nature is particularly appealing to him. He is always anxious to capture it on canvas, but so far he has not succeeded.

The three women laugh and chat and don't seem to feel that the painter is looking at them with his professional eye.
"So, girls, we have to start now," Antonius finally warns. "Otherwise it will get too dark.
The women quickly get rid of their clothes and are willingly set up by the artist. Unlike Raphael, whose models touch each other only slightly at the shoulders, Antonius asks the women to snuggle up tightly. Anna, with her protruding buttocks, he arranges back to himself. Her red curls fall deep down and almost reach to her hips. He turns her head so that he can see her even profile. He asks her to embrace the other two and pull them to him. Lisa and Dora stand sideways to the painter and bow their heads to Anna. Lisa's lush hair falls over her shoulder as Dora's blonde splendour floods her back. All three women embrace each other. When Antonius has positioned her correctly, he pulls out a narrow, long strip of woven fur with a leopard pattern. He skilfully drapes it around the women, so that they could be loosely connected or tied up. After a final look at his models, the artist stands behind the canvas and begins his work.

At first he creates the figures on a flat surface and designs the composition of his work. This is easy for him to do and soon he can devote himself to the details. At first he concentrates on Anna's buttocks, which shine enticingly against him. He applies the colour of her skin in a paste-like manner and then lends it the special transparency that is characteristic of Anna's skin with glazed layers of colour. He loses himself in contemplating the luxuriant backside and lets his brush glide over the canvas again and again, as if stroking his model's bottom. Only when Dora moves does he awaken from his trance-like state. He examines his work and despite his mental absence, he has portrayed Anna's bottom well.

Only now does he realize that the three women are whispering to each other. Anna now looks over at him and then giggles and hides her face on Lisa's neck. "Should we really?" he hears Dora ask.

"Why not," is Lisa's answer. "Let's see how he reacts. Then the women separate from each other and approach Antonius. Dora takes him by the hand and pulls him over to the old-fashioned couch near the stove. She is covered with red velvet, which is very worn in some places.

"What are you doing? What are you going to do? Antonius looks around looking for help. But there is no one who can save him from the women who seem to have gone crazy.

Dora sits astride him and unbuttons his flannel shirt. Lisa just takes off his right shoe and Anna has put on his beret and ruffles his dark curls.

"But girls," the painter defends himself weakly.

In the twinkling of an eye, the women have stripped the painter and begin to caress him with their bodies. Antonius does not know what is happening to him. How often has he indulged in daydreams in which he has sex with two of his models? But he never dared to make a suggestion in this direction. Of course, he has often slept with a model, for this is often inevitable when he paints a nude for many hours and the model stands in front of him in a provocative pose or lies on the couch. And never before has a woman been reluctant to give herself to him.

But what he experiences today exceeds his wildest dreams. Anna, Dora and Lisa kiss, stroke and caress him with hot hands. He can't tell which of them is holding his penis in her hand and gently massaging his testicles. Is it Lisa who kisses the bicep of his right arm and then nibbles on it with her teeth? His head seems to rest in Anna's lap as red curls fall over his eyes and block his view. So he can't even guess which of the women will sit on him and insert his penis into him. But whoever rides him, she does it gently and tenderly.

Nevertheless, Antonius finally decides to take the lead. He fumbles around with his hands until he feels the soft flesh of thighs. As a painter he is very familiar with anatomy and follows the inside of the thigh to his shame. There he uses his index finger to find his way inside and begins a rhythmic massage that produces a loud groan. With his other hand he finds a breast which he gently caresses. When his rider releases him, he straightens up in a flash and, since Anna's hair no longer obstructs his view, can oversee his position. It must have been Dora who sat on him, for she is now making Lisa a sign to do the same. But Antonius has other plans. With a firm grip he forces Lisa next to him and quickly lies down on her. Since she willingly opens her thighs, he quickly penetrates her and begins to move inside her. He takes his time and pushes her slowly, because he wants to enjoy sex with the three women as long as possible. But then he hears Anna's voice.

"Not so long', she sulks, 'I also want to sleep with you, Antonius!

Then the artist withdraws from Lisa.

When he turns to Anna, he notices the heavy musk scent that she exudes.

"But I want you from behind, Anna," he says. "I love your wonderful ass.

Anna agrees at once and Antonius stretches out her luxuriant bottom towards her. He quickly penetrates her and now slowly loses his restraint. While he sleeps with Anna, Dora mimics him and strokes first his backside to then deal with his testicles.

"I love your wonderful ass," she whispers and laughs. "And your beautiful testicles, too."

Soon after he feels her mouth on his scrotum.

Antonius moans now loudly and behaves like wild.

Lisa has crouched down in front of him so that he looks directly at her pussy.

"Come Antonius," she lures. "Kiss me!"

The painter makes a weak attempt, but before he can

stick his tongue between Lisa's labia, he comes, much to the women's regret.

"Already over," Lisa shouts. "What a pity!

"You can't do that to us, Antonius!" Dora says and pouts.

Only Anna is satisfied. She purrs like a cat and doesn't want to let Antonius leave her.

"Give me a break, girl. Then we can try it again," the artist tries to comfort the girls.

"No, there's no break here," says Dora. "Lisa help me to bring him up again!

And already the women start to raise Antonius' penis again.

In the meantime it has become dark in the studio. The embers in the small oven hiss just before they go out completely. The moon shines through the little window and throws her faint light on the ball of naked bodies of people, who are occupied with each other on the worn couch as if in an endless game.

The picture of the three Graces must probably wait a little while for its completion.

The Beloved Professor

Manuela was sitting with her little daughter Ina in the consultation room of Prof. Bachmann, as so often in the last year. Ina had a complicated bladder weakness and was therefore treated in the urology department of the hospital. Once a week Manuela had to come with her to uroflowmetry, which always took her quite some time. Ina was hard to get to drink enough fluid and it took a long time before she could pee and have her urine flow measured. Manuela had already given her many tasty drinks to animate her and now they had arrived at malt beer. That had worked and Ina had drunk enough. The uroflowmetry was done and now they were waiting for Prof. Bachmann, who wanted to discuss the results with her as usual.

The professor was a very pleasant man. He was no longer young - Manuela estimated him to be in his mid-fifties - his dark hair was streaked with grey threads. But his curved eyebrows were of a deep black and very eye-catching in the angular face with the pale skin. The professor's eyes were dark and lively, but overall he made a reworked impression. And he certainly was. He operated from morning to afternoon and then held his private consultation until late at night. It was a mystery to Manuela how he still found time to look after his students.

For several weeks Manuela noticed that the professor not only saw her as the mother of his little patient, but also looked at her with blatant interest. He praised her for reading Ina so patiently and winked at her as he opened the door to his consulting room to invite in patients ahead of Ina. It had also happened that he had given Manuela a brief insight into his private life by telling him about his daughter or his wife, who were both doctors, one in Switzerland and the other in France.
Manuela imagined the professor's life to be quite bleak. The strenuous work in the clinic and in the evening he came to an empty house. He had also once told her that he often had no time from morning until evening to eat something and that after work he went to a snack bar, very close to Manuela's house.
Oh, he will have a lover, she had thought more often.

A man like him will not remain alone. There are certainly plenty of opportunities for him. Since she was happily married herself, Prof. Bachmann only interested her when she came to his office. Afterwards she quickly forgot him.

Now Manuela and Ina sat in front of the professor's big desk and waited. Manuela had dressed nicely, because secretly she was flattered by the professor's interest. She also wanted to give him a little pleasure with the sight of her, to be a colourful mosaic stone in his grey clinic routine. Manuela wore a short mini skirt made of brown fabric and a light, slightly transparent blouse with a deep neckline. Her brown chin-length hair was cleverly cut. It ran asymmetrically around her beautiful head, started very short on the right ear and ended in a veritable flood of curls on the left side. She wore an eye-catching earring on the right, made of orange chopsticks of thin shells, which rustled mysteriously with every slight movement of her head. She had a pretty figure and beautiful legs and she was well aware of her attractiveness.

When the professor entered, Manuela tightened her back and pretended to be interested in a book on urology that had been lying on her desk. In truth, however, she had not read a word. She was eager not to miss the moment when the professor would enter. Now she looked up as if she had come from far away. She gave the professor an enchanting look and smile. "I'm sorry you had to wait so long again," the professor apologized and shook her hand. "Once again there was a lot going on today and then an emergency came up."

"But that doesn't matter," Manuela replied. "Ina and I always have enough to read with. Haven't we, Ina?

The child nodded. The child was always a little intimidated when Prof. Bachmann came into the room. It probably felt like its mother the strong presence the professor radiated. For Manuela, the urologist seemed integer, but a little dominant. He was a leader, you could feel it immediately. He always seemed to know what he wanted and he pushed it through.

This is probably the basic prerequisite for a career as a doctor, Manuela was thinking about it when the professor approached her again.

"You are interested in urology, Mrs. Wagner?"

"Inevitably," Manuela replied with a hint to her daughter. "But please excuse me. It was rude of me to just take the book."

"You can borrow it. I have another copy."

Manuela did not answer. She just smiled at the professor. He turned to Ina and asked her a few questions. During a short ultrasound examination, during which Manuela held Inas hand, Prof. Bachmann grazed her hand with his arm. Manuela felt a shiver run through her.

What is the matter with me today, she asked herself. Why does the professor have such an attraction for me?

She couldn't explain it to herself. She felt scratched up and as awake and alive as she had not felt for a long time.

But he is also a beautiful man, she thought. If I were not married, I would try to seduce him. He is exactly the man who suits me.

But then the examination was over. The professor handed her the patient file and sent her to the antechamber.

"Please hand it over, Ina," he said and the child ran off immediately.

"Just a moment, Mrs. Wagner. May I ask you something?

Manuela was alarmed. She looked at the professor with a little skepticism. What would come now? But then he already spoke.

"You know that I often go to this snack bar in the evening?

Manuela nodded. "Yes, why?

"Today I just don't feel like it. I would like to go to a restaurant and eat something good. Would you like to accompany me?"

"Yes, that's a nice idea," Manuela heard herself say.

"That's nice. Can you pick me up in front of the clinic at 8:15? Then I should be done here. If I don't come immediately, please wait for me. I will definitely come."

When they shook hands, a spark jumped over.

"By the way, I love your perfume and still notice it when you and Ina are long gone. May I ask which one it is?

"Este Lauder's private collection," she replied.

Manuela was like in a trance. What had she done? She couldn't possibly have dinner with Prof. Bachmann in the evening? She was married and had to put the children to bed at that time. And yet she already knew that she would somehow make it possible.

There was already no turning back for her.

Punctually at eight o'clock Manuela stood with her car in the patients' parking lot of the clinic and it only took a few minutes until she saw the professor, who approached her with a dynamic step. He opened the passenger door and got in unbiased.

It's not the first time he's done this, Manuela shot it through her head.

"Where are you going," she asked a little intimidated.

"Is an Italian all right with you," Prof. Bachmann asked.

Shortly afterwards they found themselves at a table in an Italian restaurant.

"I think we should not address each other so formally," the professor said by the way and studied the menu. "My name is Ulf and you are Manuela, right?

"Manu, they call me Manu."

"What would you like to eat, Manu?"

Ulf ate fast and hastily. It was clear that he was very hungry. Then he calmed down and cheered to Manuela with his red wine. He took her hand in his and looked deep into her eyes.

"You surely know how much I like you," he asked. "For some time now I have been getting very restless when I see you and Ina sitting in my waiting room. And for a few weeks now I've been searching the appointment book every morning for Inas name and when I see you coming in the afternoon my day is saved. I look forward to this moment all day long." Manuela felt flattered, even though she couldn't believe what the professor said. Why her of all people? And did he mean to say that he had fallen in love with her?

"I think I fell in love with you," Ulf said at the same moment.

Can he read minds, Manuela asked herself confused. "And you? Do you like me a little too?

"Yes, I do. I have also been attracted to you for some time. I just don't know if it has anything to do with love."

"Yes, with what else?

"I think with eroticism. That now sounds strange, but I love my husband and my children, just as you love your wife. So this attraction can only be erotic, right?"

"No matter what we want to call this feeling," Ulf replied, "It is there and wants to be lived. Let's go."

They drove back to the clinic. There he led her up to the urological department on the 11th floor of the clinic. It was very quiet here now. Only an emergency light was on and the operating rooms were unlit. There were no patients here. The ward with the patient rooms was one floor lower.

Ulf suddenly stopped on the long corridor, as if something had just occurred to him. He turned to Manu, who had followed him wordlessly so far.

"Come here," he whispered and pulled her into his arms.

He held her for a few seconds and moaned comfortably, as if he had finally gotten something long desired. Then he kissed her. At first he was timid, then more and more demanding. His hands wandered over her body. He pressed her onto her buttocks and gently grasped her breasts. Manu let herself fall into these caresses and was all the more shocked when Ulf suddenly released her.

"Come," he said again, pulling Manu's hand behind him. Purposefully, he opened the door of an examination room and pulled her into it with him. In the darkness of the room - only the scattered light from outside illuminated it a little - Manu saw a treatment chair similar to that of her gynaecologist.

"Will you examine me?" she jokingly asked.

"Something like that," Ulf gave back quite seriously. He toiled with a few switches, conjured up a diffuse light in the room and finally switched on the light he used to examine his patients' urethras and bladders. Then he pulled white crepe paper from a roll fastened behind the chair and stretched it across the chair down to the seat. Now he took a white coat from a wall hook and grazed it. Finally he put on a mouth and nose mask, as he used to do during surgeries. He also did not do without the latex gloves. Only now did he turn back to Manu.

"What's that all about? What are we doing here?
Manuela laughed embarrassedly.

The answer was "playing doctor and patient".

Ulf led her to the edge of the chair. Here he began to pull the dress over her head and to remove her panties. Manu unlocked the clasp of her bra himself. She was quite excited by the abstruse situation she was in with Ulf. Until a few hours ago Ulf had been a respected professor for her!

Trembling with lust, she waited to see what Ulf would do next. He sat down on his small wheelchair and grabbed Manu by the hips. Slowly, as if tasting the precious seconds of excitement, he approached her breasts with his mouth and began to explore and caress them extensively with his tongue.

"Sit down," he ordered all of a sudden. "And put your legs here on the supports.

Manuela obeyed, climbed a bit awkwardly onto the chair and put one leg each on the right and left into the supports provided for it. Now she was completely at Ulf's mercy. The latter pointed the lamp at her pubic region and clicked his tongue with the air of an expert. "Very nice," he said. "Young and firm. As I love it."

And he bent down, examined a few seconds extensively Manuela`s vagina and then sank his head between her legs. Now he excited her clitoris with his tongue and only when she cried out with pleasure did he raise his head and start to finger her vulva. She felt the cold latex on her skin, but instead of being repelled, she felt shivers of lust. Ulf spread her now, penetrated her with two rubber fingers and gave her more lust. Finally he also was beside himself with lust. He opened his coat and the trousers under it and before Manuela realized, he had already penetrated her. Now he took her very fast and hard and it took only a few minutes until he reached his climax. He apologized for his impatience and asked Manuela to stay as she was.

"I'll just pour us a little red wine," he said and went over to a cupboard.

Manuela meanwhile took her legs off the supports and straightened up. She was a little dizzy. Everything had gone so fast and she had not been prepared for such a situation. She would never have dreamed of ever having sex on an examination chair. This had nothing to do with the harmless role plays of her childhood. That was eroticism of a special kind.

Ulf approached her smiling with two filled wine glasses.

"Don't get off, Manu!" he ordered. "We're not finished yet. Once I've had a few sips of wine, it'll be stiff again. You will see that I am very persevering the second and third time".

Manuela smiled and they cheered to each other.

"You are very imaginative," Manuela tried to praise Ulf.

"Do you like it?" he asked. "I thought to myself that you were receptive to this game.

"Do you play it often?

"Yes, but only in my imagination. I've been waiting for you to put it into reality."

Manuela didn't believe a word he said. She saw herself

in a row with nurses, students and patients who had all been seduced in a similar way by Professor Bachmann. But she didn't mind. She did not love this man and had no ownership rights over him. He might sleep with whomever he wanted, if only she was there from time to time.

As promised, the professor recovered quickly and asked Manuela to sit back in position.

She had barely laid her legs on the supports when the professor took two short braided plastic straps out of his coat pocket and tied Manuela's legs to the supports. Then he took two more straps from the bag and fixed her arms to the backrests. She had already been the passive at the first act because of her position, but now she was completely incapable of acting. There was nothing left for her to do but let Ulf do with her whatever he wants. He began again to give her pleasure in different ways, sometimes with his tongue, sometimes with his fingers. Yes, he even went so far as to mate her with the attachment of the ultrasound device. Manuela let everything happen to her and sometimes she reared up with lust. Three more times Ulf penetrated her with his penis and took her hard and demanding. Then he seemed exhausted and satisfied. He kissed her on the mouth and unbuttoned the ligaments on her arms. Freed from this, Manuela put her arms around his neck and pressed herself firmly against him.

"Thank you," she breathed.

"It was wonderful," he gave back.

From that evening on, Manuela was always looking for

reasons why she couldn't be home in the evening. Sometimes she wanted to go to the cinema with a friend, other times she met former colleagues and she started jogging in the evening. But in reality she went to Ulf's clinic every time. She had a wonderful time with him until one day he told her that his wife had given up her job in Switzerland and would start at his clinic as a pediatrician.

This meant the end of Manuela's turbulent relationship with Ulf, whom she now loved seriously. She became very sad and he also regretted that her creative sexual role plays had come to an end.

"I will never forget you," he promised on her last evening. "You have given me so much.

But the worst thing was that Ina, Manuela's daughter, still had to go to Prof. Bachmann for an examination. What torture it meant for Manuela to sit in front of Ulf's desk and don't let on anything. How much she would have liked to fling her arms around his neck and confessed her love to him. But for her daughter's sake, she had to control herself and she was happy when she was finally healthy and the consultations with Prof. Bachmann were no longer necessary.

After Inas last examination, the professor held Manuela back for a moment in the examination room. "As always, please bring the file card to the front room," he gave Ina one last order.

Ina immediately left the room and ran to the secretary's office. In the meantime she knew her way around the ward well.

The professor took Manuela one last time tenderly in

his arms and kissed her.

"I love you," said Manuela. "And I will never forget you. Will you sometimes think of me too?

"I will stay connected with you, come what may. But unfortunately only in my heart. You know that this is the last time we will see each other.

The two lovers pressed each other's hands and Manuela left the examination room. She was never to see her beloved professor again.

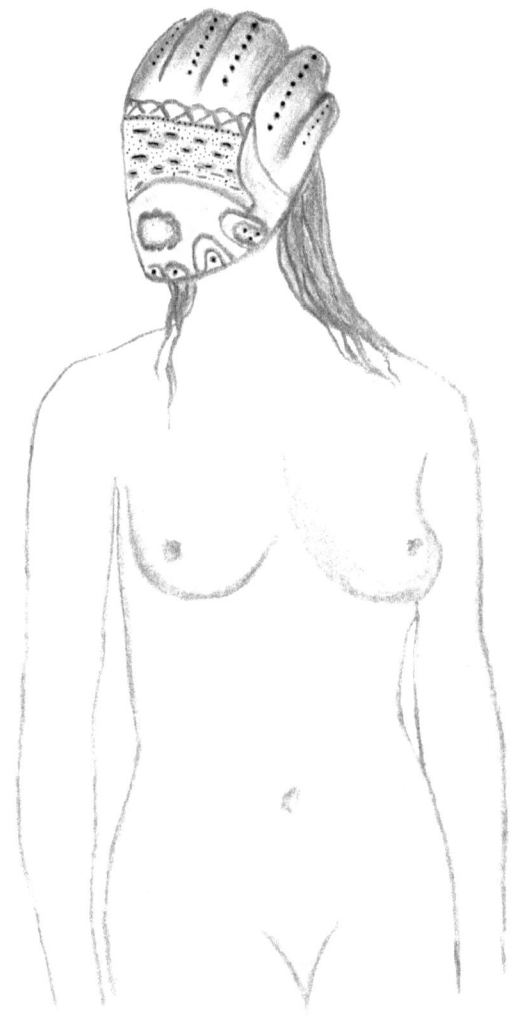

75

The House of the faceless Women

I sat in my black Porsche and watched my wife leave the editorial office where she worked as a journalist and cross the street. As always, Esther was elegantly dressed. Over her short brown skirt she wore a jade-coloured cashmere twinset. Her coat of beaver fur was open and every step revealed the view of her long legs in high suede boots. It was winter, but on a clear day like this, the midday sun created a cheerful atmosphere.

Esther entered a flower shop. When she appeared at the door again, she had twenty dark red roses in her arms. She came up to my car, which I had parked in front of the editorial office to pick her up, opened the door and carefully stowed the bouquet behind the passenger seat. Ester got in and we drove home. We lived in a fancy old apartment in the centre of the city. I worked as a freelance photographer. I got my commissions from agencies and so I could freely dispose of my time. I often supported Esther when she needed gripping photos for a story in her magazine.

"I told you about the doctor who is involved in illegal human trafficking," Esther said on our way home. "Do you remember?"

I nodded.

"I think I'm slowly getting behind his secret. But I really need solid evidence before I can write the story."

"And you were thinking about photos, right?"

"Guessed. I made an appointment with the doctor for tonight. You do have time, don't you?"

"Well, not necessarily, but I think I can make it for you."

"You're a sweetheart," she said and kissed me on the cheek.

Half an hour later Esther drove her car across a lonely country road. I sat next to her. The bag with my photo equipment stood at my feet. We hadn't seen a house for quite a while. It was pitch-black. A weather front was pulled up and deep black clouds covered the sky. Only in one place they were diffusely illuminated. Only the moon could hide behind it.

While Esther was looking for the house, which had to emerge every moment from the darkness, I observed a grand spectacle in the sky. At the lower edge of a large cloud a narrow crescent moon appeared. It hung there like a swing, as one sees it otherwise only on the southern hemisphere. Then the cloud released the full moon. It looked like a thick drop of liquid silver threatening to fall to the earth. But a few seconds later the moon was hidden behind the next cloud. Esther meanwhile steered the car into a narrow dirt road, at the end of which an old, large house stood lonely on a hill. With its square shape and the columns in front of the entrance, the house looked like a castle from a historical film. It was only dimly lit. Obviously all curtains were closed.

"Are you sure we're on the right track," I asked.

"Quite sure. I'm waiting for you here. It is better if you go alone. He should be very shy.

"But you arranged the appointment with him.

"I pretended to be your secretary."

"Oh so. See you soon then. The house looks quite scary.

With these words I left the car.

I walked towards the great wrought-iron gate. A servant asked my name and opened it for me. He accompanied me to the imposing front door, which opened after a short ring. Before me stood a man in a black suit. He had a colorful silk scarf around his neck. I introduced myself and casually mentioned that my wife was waiting for me in the car. I can't remember why I did that, but a vague restlessness drove me to it. I wanted the doctor to know that I had not come alone.

"Come in," said the old man friendly. "We don't want to let your pretty wife wait unnecessarily long.

He closed the door behind me and turned the key.

"Just a precaution," he said shrugging his shoulders as he caught my questioning gaze.

He led me into an anteroom. There, in a vase on a pedestal, stood a thick bouquet of red, long-stemmed roses that looked a little faded.

"You can put your coat here," he said, pointing his hand to a wardrobe where many dark coats were already hanging.

I noticed that the doctor's hands were as thin as a skeleton. They were wrinkled and covered with pigment spots. The swanky golden signet ring on the right ring finger seemed completely out of place.

"Come," the old man said, "I want to show you something."

He pushed me through a door and I was instantly blinded by bright light. Muffled music filled the spacious room to which other rooms seemed to connect. I didn't believe my eyes. The room was furnished with a series of armchairs and sofas, all precious pieces of furniture with covers of seemingly precious fabrics. The high windows were darkened with red velvet curtains and various floor lamps spread a soft light. In the room it was very quiet, nobody spoke a loud word. Only a general murmur could be heard.

All this did not fit to what I saw. About a dozen naked young women were fucked before my eyes in all imaginable positions by one or more men. On an armchair sat a fat old man who had opened his shirt. He had stripped off his trousers and they were hanging above his expensive leather shoes. A naked young woman squatted on him. The man held her by the hips with both hands and helped her to slide up and down his penis. I was shocked and did not notice for the time being what irritated me most about what I saw.

But then I suddenly realized that the woman was wearing a hood. It was made of brocade fabric and apparently embroidered with precious pearls. And it had no openings for the eyes. Only there, where the mouth was, the hood had a round opening and two tiny holes in the height of the nose. I felt reminded of the performance of a falconer I had recently watched. The falconer had put hoods like these on the birds to keep them quiet as long as they were sitting on the bar. What did that mean? Shouldn't the woman see who she gave herself to during sex? Did the fat man want to remain unrecognised because he was a well-known personality? I looked closer. The man was similar to a member of the city council, but I wasn't sure.

Now I saw that all the women in the room wore similar hoods.

What's the point, I was just wondering, when I discovered a well-known politician. He just took a woman from behind who had bent over the armrest of one of the sofas. Next to this couple was another man sitting on the sofa. He was much younger than most of us here, almost all of whom were already old. The man who was in his forties wore a silk dressing gown which he had opened wide. Before him a naked woman knelt on a golden pillow and had the man's phallus in her mouth.

So that's what the round hole in the hood was for, I thought.

Behind the woman an elderly gentleman in red

underpants knelt and worked on the woman's shame with his tongue.

Silk cushions were scattered on the floor in a corner of the room. There lay a naked man with an erect penis and a young woman in each arm. He was busy satisfying the two dazzled beauties. The fingers of his left hand were playing with the clitoris of one, while his right hand was kneading the lush breasts of the other. One of the women had just reached for the man's penis and began massaging it.

I only had one wish. I wanted to get out of this house and back to my wife's car as soon as possible. I had long forgotten the photos I was supposed to take for her.

And it certainly wouldn't have been a good idea to take pictures here.

Just when I wanted to turn to the door, a servant in a monk's robe brought a woman to me. She had curly blonde hair that poured out from under the hood and over her narrow shoulders. Her skin was very soft and she had a perfect figure. Narrow hips, slender waist and small firm breasts. But the most beautiful thing about her was her long, slender legs. She wore, like all other women here, high heeled shoes. These and the brocade hoods were the only clothes the women seemed allowed to wear.

"For you," said the doctor. "Help yourself. You can do whatever you want with her. She will be at your service with everything."

Before I could answer anything, I did not want to

accept this immoral offer, the woman took my hand in silence and continued. She walked calmly with me through the room I had seen from the door. We walked past the couples who were so busy with each other that they took no notice of us. As I walked by, I recognized many a gentleman who had come before my lens during my work as a photographer. Mostly local politicians, but also businessmen and doctors. On a couch, the head of the children's clinic lay in close embrace with two women. I was horrified by the secret double lives of all these men, who always seemed to have such integrity in public.

The young woman led me into another room that was just as pompously furnished. We walked over thick soft carpets to a chaise longue covered with old pink velvet. There the woman sat down, leaned back casually and spread her thighs. I wondered how she had found her way here so safely. Could she see anything through her bonnet? I made a test by taking my camera out of the cover and holding it right in front of her face. She didn't protest, so I was sure she couldn't see anything. Reflexively I pressed the shutter button, even though I suspected that it was not advisable to photograph here. But at least I had come here with this job. My wife was waiting for me outside in the car and she was dependent on the evidence photos I was supposed to take.

Nevertheless, I did not dare to turn around and photograph the man who was sleeping with a young woman near me. I packed my camera again and looked down on the playmate who had been made available to me. What should I do now? Should I help myself to her and then leave the house and forget everything as quickly as possible?

You make yourself complicit, my conscience announced itself. These women are certainly not here voluntarily. I suspected that the young women had been given drugs. Otherwise they would not be so apathetic about all these sex games. Nowhere else could you hear the silly laughter that is so often heard with prostitutes. The women also did not drink alcohol, while the men had all glasses of whisky or cognac next to them on small tables. The servants in the frocks kept walking around and filling up the glasses. Nobody noticed them. It seemed indifferent to the men that the servants could watch them with their playmates. Even the men among each other, who certainly met more often in public, took no offence at being seen by each other.

While I was still thinking about all this, the woman stood up in front of me and groped for me. She found my belt and opened it. Then she pulled up my zipper and slipped my trousers and underpants down. She looked with her hand for my penis, found it and began to massage it. In a matter of seconds he straightened up to an amazing size. Only now did I feel how excited I was to be touched by a woman who obviously couldn't see me and whose face remained hidden to me. I was tempted for a moment to pull off her grotesque cap with the round mouthhole, but at the same moment a hot wave of lust carried me away and I just enjoyed being seduced by the woman. As in ecstasy I threw my photo equipment on the ground. I pulled me the shirt over the head and threw me on the beauty who had still spread the thighs far. I penetrated into her without any consideration and took her with such greed, as if I had not had sex for years. She allowed everything I wanted from her. She let me take her from behind and sat down on me as a matter of course when I expressed this wish. She rode me in a fast gallop and let me hear a restrained moaning. Suddenly a second woman joined us on the chaise longue. Also she was blond, but her hair was smooth and long. She began, while the other woman rode me, to nibble at my earlobes and breathed obscene words into my ear. I was close to going crazy with excitement. Then the woman suddenly called my name and I instantly found myself back in reality. I knew this voice. I looked up at the woman, but her face was protected from my eyes by the hood. But I was alarmed. Gently I lifted the other one from my penis. "Wait a minute," I said panting.

She obeyed and sat quietly beside me. Now I had the opportunity to look at the second woman and what I saw drove me again the sweat on the forehead. This time not with pleasure, but with disbelieving horror. The woman next to me was my wife, I was sure of that now.

"Esther,' I exclaimed in horror. "What are you doing here?

"I just wanted to see whether you were having a good time too," she returned unmoved.

"What does that mean? Why did you send me here?
"I finally wanted to open your eyes," she replied.
"Open your eyes? What do you mean by that?
"What do you think I used to pay for the new Porsche? And where do you think the money for the trip to Australia comes from? You can't have seriously believed that I would make so much money as a journalist."
"You work here," I asked in horror.
"Sometimes, when I feel like it, I also work here with the men," she returned. "But actually I'm already too old for that. You see, the girls here are all still quite young, grown-up, but young."
I looked over at her in amazement and wished she would take off the silly hood. The hole in the mouth seemed to mock me in its obscenity.
"I am the doctor's accomplice. We built this together. I was his mistress for a while, but now we're just business partners," she continued.
I didn't want to hear all this. Her talk seemed too cruel to me. All this could only be a bad dream!
"I lured you here so that you would finally notice something, you idiot," Esther now gave me a nasty smack. "Because I've had enough of you for a long time. You bore me, do you know that?
I just looked at her in a dumbfounded way, unable to answer anything.
"So and now I go', she said. "I wish you much more pleasure. If you like, I can send you a second girl. If I were you, I would take advantage of this today. A second time you will not have the opportunity. You

have no idea how much money the men here pay for one night."

With these words she got up and went over to an obese man who was having fun with a woman on a sofa. She patted the woman on the shoulder and she climbed down from the man and walked away. My wife took the free seat, sat astride the man and inserted his penis. Then she began to ride it before my eyes. In order not to have to look at this, I turned again to my little one. She immediately spread her legs and let me come to her. Angrily I took her, did not hold me back with the orgasm and moaned loudly. I wanted my wife to hear it, but she was much too busy because a second man had joined her, kissing her buttocks while she was still riding on the fat one. Soon another woman came to me and I tried to forget everything in the embrace of the two beautiful ones. At times I succeeded, but the pain over my wife's infidelity was deep. And had it not been more than sexual infidelity? Esther thought I was a failure. She didn't believe in me as a photographer and she had yelled at me that I was boring her. Why hadn't she told me all this before? Why did she let me believe that we had a good marriage? I could not understand it. And all the sex in the world was not enough to comfort me from this grief. So I soon freed myself from the embrace of the young beauties and left the house. As I walked through the vestibule, I noticed that the roses had been exchanged for fresh ones.

As if in a trance, I ran to our Porsche and sat inside. Then my eyes fell on the passenger seat on which the paper was lying, in which the red roses Esther had bought were wrapped. That was the proof. I hadn't dreamed. The house with the faceless women did not only exist in my imagination. I started the engine and drove back to the country road. There, in the solitude of the night, I accelerated the car as high as I could and hoped that I would not survive the trip to the city.

Cose della vita

Ciao, I'm Claudio. I must tell you a story. You won't
believe what happened to me the other day.
I am a pizza delivery boy. But actually I am a student. I
study Applied Geosciences at the RWTH Aachen. Or
rather, I studied, because I'm still enrolled, but haven't
been attending lectures for a year. Lena is to blame for
that. She left me and the motivation was over. But
that's another story.

Now I'm a pizza delivery boy, which means I'm
actually a dressman and a model. With my distinctive
Roman face and the black thick curls I should actually
be sought after in this profession. But I am not. The
reason: I am too long and too thin, a real gawky guy.
Just magro come un grissino.
Nevertheless I sometimes get a request for a fashion
show. And I find that I look good in the fancy suits.
Hair gelled back, 3-day beard sharply shaved to

contour. Male, sexy and a bit bold. Also photo agencies ask me. But they always only want portraits of me. But all this is not enough for life. That's why I go out for pizzas.

But now to the story I want to tell you.

It was on a wet and cold Saturday just before Christmas. I had been on duty for four hours and had already delivered several pizzas when my boss sent me to an address I knew. The house I was supposed to go to was a skyscraper and the elevator was often broken there. I hate this house because I have neither the time nor the desire to climb many floors to deliver two pizzas. Most people are lazy and don't meet you. So I was already in a bad mood on the way there. Most of the time I sing Italian songs like Più Bella Cosa and things like that in my Fiat. But on this trip "niente"! Arriving at the skyscraper, I stuck the bill between my teeth, opened the trunk, took out the warming box and sneaked to the house to look for the bell. I found the name Neumann at the top.

"Madre Mio," I moaned. "Hopefully the elevator will work."

It did, and I drove up, sending a quick prayer to heaven. A woman in her thirties leaned in the open apartment door. Not beautiful, but pretty with long brown hair and lively eyes.

"Hello," she said in a sticky sweet manner.

"For Neumann," I asked indifferently.

"Would you please take it to the kitchen," the woman asked. "I have a little something for you for Christmas.

I mumbled something in Italian and entered the apartment.

"Right here on the right," said the woman. "What's your name?

"Claudio. Where to put it?

She pointed to the table and when I had unpacked the pizzas, she actually gave me a small parcel. It was wrapped in nice Christmas paper and weighed about 200 grams.

"I hope you'll like it," said the woman smiling.

Now I became a little friendlier. I thanked her and was about to cash when she said: "Claudio, don't you want to stay here and eat with us. You look as if you haven't eaten for a long time."

"That's deceiving," I replied. "I was always so thin.

"But you are tired," she said. "Come sit with us in the living room for a few minutes and have a sip of red wine. My girlfriend and I like to share with you".

And she took my hand and pulled me into the living room. There sat a second pretty bride. Blond, blue-eyed and with a big mouth.

"Ciao Bello," she said and laughed at me broadly.

"Maxi, Claudio", we were introduced. "And my name is Kati."

The women invited me to sit on the couch. Kati had put the pizzas on plates and brought them in.

"Reach out," she challenged me, but I didn't react. As a pizza delivery boy, I can no longer smell pizzas and certainly not eat them. But I gladly accepted the red wine.

The two girls stuck one piece of pizza after the other

in their mouths and it seemed to taste good to them. Suddenly Kati jumped up and went into the kitchen. I heard the fridge door and she shouted: "I still have a steak, Claudio. Shall I fry it for you?

I didn't say no. But I had hardly swallowed the first bite when my phone rang. My boss wanted to know where I was. But since I didn't feel like jumping up immediately and continuing working, I lied to him. "Scusi, Capo, I have a car breakdown. It's going to take a while."

My boss raved at the other end and I held the mobile far away from my ear.

The women laughed and I gave them signs to be calm. The steak tasted excellent, just like the broccoli Kati had warmed up. I felt well. It was cosy and warm in the apartment and the discreet Christmas decoration made her very comfortable.

When the pizzas and the steak had been eaten, Kati turned to me and asked: "Well, you want some dessert?

"Yes, that would be nice," I replied.

Then Kati opened her blouse, pushed her bra up and exposed her firm round breasts right in front of my eyes.

"Mama mia", I said and looked at the beautiful curves. "Don't be shy, Claudio. You may touch her calmly", Kati whispered.

And I did. I kneaded and sucked on it while Kati glided deep into the pads. From the corner of my eye I noticed that Maxi was beginning to undress.

What is this supposed to be, I asked myself just as I

felt Kati's finger nesting on the zipper of my jeans. Shortly afterwards she pulled down my trousers and underpants with a jerk.

"Oh, santi numi," I moaned and immediately felt Kati's hand on my stiff penis. She did the same thing with it as I did with her breasts before. And, yes, she finally took it in her mouth. I leaned back and let it happen.

Why not, I thought. Since Lena left me, my sex life has not looked so rosy. Why shouldn't I just let Kati do it? But I didn't quite get the chance to enjoy the fellatio, because next to me Maxi was whining and tugging at my sweater.

"I also want dessert," she said and sulked.

"Yes, immediately, Chicca," I comforted her and grabbed her breast with my right hand, which was still in a red lace bra.

I tried to get my fingers under the lace, but I didn't succeed.

"Get undressed," I said and turned back to Kati, who was sitting on me.

Maxi obeyed and took off her thong, which she had kept on for whatever reason.

"Come here," I asked her.

I prevented Kati from sitting on my phallus and asked her to undress first.

Then my phone rang. My boss called again. He shouted at me. Where I was he wanted to know, what he should do, who do I think, should do my work...

"I sprained my foot, boss', I lied. "He is quite stiff and the customer from Hermanngasse is treating him right now. It'll take a while, but I'll come as soon as I'm done here."

Maxi and Kati were bursting with laughter behind their hands.

The break that had occurred had been enough for the women to undress completely. I also got rid of my hooded shirt and took off my trousers and shoes. But what should I do now with the two women who both looked at me expectantly? To serve two Ragazzis as a man is not so easy, I feared. I remembered a sex film I saw many years ago. I asked Kati to lie on her back and Maxi to sit astride her. The girls did what I wanted and I kneeled behind them. Man, how awesome was that? I could choose which of them I wanted to penetrate. Into Kati in the missionary position or into Maxi in the doggy position. Both pussies lay almost directly on top of each other. And so I helped myself, penetrated once into Maxi, which I held at the hips and then again into Kati, whose thighs I spread with my hands. And while I tried to serve both women equally, they kneaded each other's breasts.

In order not to come immediately and enjoy this ride as long as possible, I tried to think in between of the boring sex with Lena. We had actually never really had fun, had always slept together in the same position. That really turned me off and so I stood my ground for quite a long time. I do not know how often I changed from one pussy to the other. When I was in Kati, Maxi complained that I should come back to her quickly and vice versa. But finally I exploded. Even the best Italian won't last that long!

Exhausted I slipped down from the women and the couch and remained sitting on the carpet with my limbs stretched far from me.

The women also had to take their breath, but were not yet satisfied. They crawled down to me and started massaging and stroking me.

But I resisted.

"I cannot, Chiccas. You have heard, my boss is waiting for me. If I don't get into business soon, I'll be out of a job."

They wouldn't let me go and I had to promise to come back as soon as possible. And I gladly promised that.

"Do you have a bandage?" I asked Kati. "I must bandage my stiff foot so that the boss will believe me.

Kati went to the bathroom and came back with an elastic bandage that she wanted to wrap around my penis for fun. Maxi had a fit of laughter.

What crazy chickens they are, I thought.

Then I wrapped the bandage around my left foot and got dressed.

To say goodbye I kissed both women extensively, took my insolating box and ran down the stairs.

On the way back to the pizzeria I beltet out "Cose della vita" and decided not to let life get me down again.

Hot Nights on Mallorca

During my last holiday on Mallorca I met a young man
on the beach. I lay on my beach sheet and dozed in
the sun in front of me. The last night in the disco had
been very long. My friend Jessica, with whom I spent
the holiday, had such a bad headache that she had to
stay in bed. She had probably drunk one Bacardi too
much. The sun warmed my back. I was feeling
comfortable and thought of a colleague with whom I
had spent some hot office hours in the last few weeks.

Suddenly something soft landed on my back.
Frightened, I turned around and looked into the
tanned face of a young man laughing towards me.
"Sorry, no intention. My buddy over there is still
practicing," he said grinning, pointing to his friend,
who was as well-built as he was.
"It's okay,' I said. "Fortunately, it was just a softball.

95

I was pleased to see that he looked fascinated at my naked breasts.

I have big, beautifully shaped breasts, and I'm used to men being magically attracted to them. I always take the offensive right away. It's just fun for me to shock the boys.

"Don't you like them?" I asked and put on a pout.

"Oh yes" he stammered embarrassed. "It's just because they're so..."

He broke off his sentence in the middle.

"You mean because they're so big."

"Yes, exactly. Bye then!"

He was suddenly in a hurry. With a few leaps forward he was back with his playing partner. For a while I watched them play, then I turned back to lie prone. I must have fallen asleep and I woke up because something tickled my ear. I opened an eye to see what disturbed me. My eyes fell on an azure bathing suit with a few hairy legs and a smooth brown belly. Abruptly I sat up.

"You fell asleep. I thought I'd wake you up. Otherwise you could get a sunburn. And that would be a pity for your beautiful skin."

"Thank you, very thoughtful of you."

After this short conversation we were both silent. The pause that arose was somehow embarrassing. I looked out at the sea, but still I watched the man next to me from the corner of my eye. He had a beautiful face. His nose was narrow and straight, his mouth big and his chin angular. He looked like a man who knows what he wants. I wondered what color his eyes might have been.

My eyes are blue and I am often told that they are very beautiful. I looked at him. At the same moment he turned his head and our eyes met.

The spark that flashed at that moment flashed through me like an electric shock.

His eyes were green and slanting. I had to think involuntarily of my tomcat Boris, who my mother took care of now. Boris is a real stray. He is often roaming the streets for nights in love affairs.

I asked myself if the cat at my side was the same.

"Will you come to the siesta with me? I'll buy you a drink," the stranger asked and interrupted my thoughts.

Since the heat was getting a little too hot for me, I got up and put on my top. Then I rolled up my beach sheet. I didn't answer.

"Well, what is. Will you come with me?

"Sure, why not?

So we set off.

It was cool in the bar. The big ceiling fan turned sluggishly. From the loudspeakers came music from the twenties. The bar was completely furnished in Art Nouveau. I liked it here. I liked the atmosphere. We drank a long drink with orange juice and gin.

"Are you on your own here?" he asked.

"No, with my friend Jessica. But she has a headache today. The disco, you understand?"

"Hm, has happened to me several times. But mostly I pay attention. It's so a pity about every day that gets lost."

In the course of the afternoon I learned that Frank, my new friend's name, was on Mallorca with his brother-in-law. We exchanged the addresses of our hotels and made an appointment for the evening. We wanted to bring our companions with us.

At eight o'clock on the dot I stood in front of the restaurant where we wanted to have a snack. I was alone, because Jessica was still not better. Frank also came without his brother-in-law.

"Jens also met a girl. He went to her hotel.

"Is he staying there?

"As I know him, I won't see him again as far as I know him. But I promised not to tell my sister anything about his escapades."

So Frank had the hotel room to himself for the night. When I thought about the possibilities we had, I was overcome by a comforting shiver. Frank seemed to have the same thought, because he smiled mischievously at me. We ate paella, but I hardly noticed how it tasted. In my mind I was already in Frank's room. We quickly got the food behind us and without talking about it we went to his hotel.

I went to the bathroom to freshen up. When I came back Frank had drawn the curtains and lay naked on the bed.

"Come Nadine," he said and stretched out his arms longingly at me.

At the sight of his muscular body I got hot. I saw that he, too, was violently aroused. Hastily I slipped out of my dress and went over to the bed. I let myself glide beside Frank on the sheet and began to kiss him. First I kissed his mouth. Then my lips glided downwards over his chest and his flat stomach to his penis, which I enclosed firmly with my mouth. Frank slowly moved his loins. He visibly enjoyed my tenderness. But suddenly he withdrew from me. Quickly he took off my knickers and put himself heavily on me. Before I could do anything, he penetrated me firmly and hard. At first he moved so fast that I thought he was going to explode. Then he seemed to reflect and moved in a lascivious rhythm that made me forget everything around me. Hot waves of lust carried me away. I smelled his skin breathing the sun of the day. I felt his strong arms holding me. I saw his green eyes and knew that he was in no way inferior to my cat. I enjoyed every one of his firm blows and was almost sad when he poured into me groaning loudly. Frank lay on me for a long time, caressed me and told me tender words. Then he rolled next to me and stroked my Venus mound. I was so excited that my body soon trembled in the highest lust.

We stayed together the night. Tired I sneaked back in to my hotel the morning .

In the early afternoon I lay again at the same place on the beach. I didn't have to wait long, and Frank showed up. He carried a big ice cream in each hand and beamed at me.

"Here, something cool for a hot lady," he said and bent over me to kiss me.

His kiss tasted good. I would have liked to give up the ice if he had kept kissing me instead. We spent the whole afternoon together. We talked, cuddled and swam a little, but not without caressing each other in secret places in the water. We had both booked a hotel with half board. And because we didn't want to miss the buffet again, everyone went back to their hotel. We agreed that I should come to Frank's room right after dinner.

I came in at half past eight. Frank stood at the window dressed only in boxer shorts and looked out. His beautiful body stood out darkly from the pale blue horizon. Silently I slipped out of my light summer dress and walked over to him naked. He must have heard me long ago, but he didn't move. I snuggled up to his back and let my nipples glide over his skin. Frank still didn't move. Only a soft sound of well-being came out of his throat. My hands glided searching over his body. I stroked his muscular chest and then slipped down into his shorts. I felt my way to the spot where I expected his bulging cock. I also found it stiff and upright in its place. But somehow it seemed smaller than yesterday. Frank groaned as I began to stroke it. Then he withdrew from my hands, turned around and smiled at me in love.
"There you are finally. I waited so longingly for you. He grabbed me by the hand and went to bed with me. I let myself fall on it immediately and lounged voluptuously. Frank took off his boxer shorts and let himself fall next to me. Because he had enjoyed it so much yesterday, I wanted to caress his penis again with my tongue. But Frank pushed me to the side. Then he

rolled over me and quickly penetrated me. Again his shocks were fast and violent. I waited patiently for the moment when, like yesterday, he would find his mastery again. But Frank rode me as if he wanted to tame me.

Suddenly he rose steeply above me. His face was distorted by the ecstasy. Loudly moaning he pushed me harder and harder and then slumped shrugging. I was surprised. What a difference to yesterday evening. Frank lay now quietly beside me and looked at me. Then he got up and went to the bathroom. When he came back he was dressed.

"I'll run down quickly," he said, "I desperately need a Coke."

With these words he disappeared and left me frustrated. Five minutes later he was back. He put the coke on the bedside table and undressed. When he lay next to me again, he pulled me tenderly into his arms. He seemed to be the old one again. His tenderness comforted me over the anger that had risen in me. Frank stroked me and then slept again with me. Now he was again the man I knew from yesterday. I attributed his strange behaviour from earlier to his unrestrained desire for me. I even felt a little flattered that I could arouse such a beautiful man so strongly.

We also spent the next nights together. I had to learn that Frank had two faces in bed. Once he was the prudent lover I had met. And another time he was closed, but wild as a bull. I never knew which Frank I would find in the hotel room. When I got out of the elevator, I tried to guess whether he would take me tenderly or relentlessly today. I was usually wet with curiosity when I walked the short way to his room.

So the most precious days of the year passed. As our vacation drew to a close, we became very sad. In Germany we lived so far away from each other that a love affair seemed impossible in the long run.

The day before the departure I went with Jessica over the beach promenade. We wanted to buy some small souvenirs for our friends at home. I was also looking for a farewell present for Frank. We strolled past the shops and entered when we were particularly interested in something. Every now and then a suggestive remark reached us, which some guy threw at us, sitting in front of one of the many pubs with a cool beer. I didn't care because I was pretty depressed. Suddenly Jessica tipped on my shoulder.

"Nadine," she said excitedly. "Look over there inconspicuously. But be prepared for something. What should there be? Probably another incredibly fat man. Jessica simply couldn't stop to bitch about other people. I turned around, but couldn't see a fat man.

"I see nothing. What do you mean?" I asked impatiently.

"Well in front! Don't you see those two?"

I searched the row of chairs standing in front of a café with my eyes. Why could Jessi never express herself clearly? But then I saw Frank. He was sitting there wearing sunglasses. There was a cocktail on the table in front of him. I was just about to call him when I saw a second Frank next to him. Confused I closed my eyes. Did I have circulatory problems? But when I opened my eyes again, there were still two Franks sitting at the table talking excitedly.

"Jessi, what does that mean?" I asked uncertainly. Jessica pulled me behind a stand with postcards.

"I don't know. They look like twin brothers." Suddenly everything became clear to me. Now I knew why Frank was so different in bed sometimes. He had sent his twin brother to me, who was probably as horny for me as Frank himself. So I had once slept with the man I had fallen in love with and then with a complete stranger. Why hadn't they been honest to me? I felt used and betrayed.

What a mean game, I thought.

Everything began to revolve around me. Jessica quickly led me away from the place of evil knowledge.

In our hotel room I cried first, then became angry with them and immediately afterwards sad again. But when I was able to think clearly again, I remembered the pleasure this confusion game had given me. I just couldn't be angry with Frank. That's why I decided to enjoy the game to the end and give the two men a lesson. Tonight I would do with the twins according to my wishes. They would be at my service. I would decide how and how often I wanted to sleep with them. And I decided to really enjoy it. I was only curious to see who of them would expect me in the hotel room.

It was Frank standing naked in front of the window. Now that my eyes had been opened, I realized that

103

there were small differences between the brothers. Frank's shoulders were a little wider than those of his brother. Only now did I notice that I didn't know his name. I had slept many times with a man who was a complete stranger to me. This thought excited me immensely. I undressed and went over to Frank. Behind him I squatted, kissed each of his tight buttocks and then crawled through his legs. When I appeared, I found myself with my mouth directly opposite his tight phallus. I greedily snapped and began to suck Frank's penis like an ice cream on a stick. Frank moaned cautiously. After a while he wanted to free himself from my mouth, but I held him with my lips. I had put both my hands on his bottom and there I exerted a certain pressure that prevented Frank from getting away from me. Now I showed him what my tongue was capable of. I closed my lips once firmly around him, then I left him a little free and played with the tongue at his glans. I sucked and smacked and Frank moaned louder and louder. Finally he began to push violently into my mouth to pour himself a little later in it. What an exciting feeling!

When we separated from each other, I said: "But now I am thirsty. Will you get me a Coke?"

Frank looked at me in amazement and I thought I saw a little mistrust in his eyes. But he put on his shorts and T-shirt and left.

The man without a name came back. He seemed to be eagerly awaiting it. He pressed the cola can wordlessly into my hand and immediately began to undress. But I did not intend to let him take me so easily. I slipped off the bed and disappeared into the bathroom. There I slowly drank my Coke and let my lover wait. Through the door gap I saw that he had sat down on the edge of the bed and played impatiently with his wristwatch. Without warning I slipped out of the bathroom and before he could react I pushed him backwards onto the bed. And I had already mounted him and started riding him in my rhythm. Now he couldn't bump into me like he was used to. I set the pace, and it was extremely slow. I glided up and down on him, soon almost completely freeing his penis to take him in shortly afterwards. Frank's brother held my big breasts tightly, just as if he wanted to hold on to them. He threw his head wildly back and forth on the mattress. I think he experienced for the first time that sex can be something other than heavy copulation. Finally he came to a climax and then lay there exhausted.

I descended from him and said almost instantly: "My God, I am thirsty today. Can you please get me another Coke?"

And so I played the game all night long. The brothers took turns with me and when one was tired, the other had recovered. I skillfully directed them into the positions I preferred and tasted everything I had so often imagined in my imagination. They took me from the front and from behind, standing and lying, on the bed and on the floor, even sitting on the toilet. So I paid them back for the deception and gave myself the most exciting night of my life.

The trick with the Coke had succeeded to them for a week, but I had seen through it and now took advantage of them shamelessly. The twins had probably not dreamed that I was so insatiable. When Frank accompanied me to the airport the next day, he looked very tired. I tenderly said goodbye to him. I didn't say a word about the fact that I knew his secret.

The Girl from the Gas Station

It's Saturday afternoon. Warm air lies over the land and the sun shines indifferently on the hilly moraine landscape. The petrol station on the B2 is lonely and deserted. Here, just behind Schmargendorf in the Uckermark, the world seems to be over. Nothing moves, no car drives by and nobody wants to refuel. This is also due to the very high gasoline prices, which for some weeks now have caused the inhabitants of the sparsely populated region to only refuel just enough to get through the next week.

Grazyna Jablonska, called Yna for short, took over the petrol station on the main road only a few months ago. In the beginning the sale went quite well and she made good additional income with the products from the gas station shop. But since the gasoline prices have risen to astronomical heights, the earning potential of the woman from the Polish town of Gryfino, which lies directly across the German/Polish border, has been declining steadily.

She is also worried about the salary of the car mechanic. Wolfgang Zwickau, whom everyone only calls Wolle, is a capable man who already worked for the previous tenant. But since a few days he has nothing more to do and is bored. He couldn't even change the oil, not to mention minor repairs.

Yna is up to her neck in trouble and is seriously worried about her existence. But she doesn't want to give up the gas station so quickly.

Why do I have such damn bad luck, she wonders. Do petrol prices have to explode right now?

The situation makes Yna sleepless and she often ponders until the early hours of the morning. But finally she comes up with a brilliant idea to save her.

Grazyna is bored, leaning against the wall between the cash desk and the car wash.

She asks herself what I was getting into, pulling the cigarette which she holds casually between her thumb and forefinger. Next to her the sign "No Smoking!" in yellow with black writing.

"You shouldn't smoke here, boss," shouts Wolle from inside. "How many times should I tell you that's dangerous?"

Yna just shrugs her shoulders and keeps smoking. Dangerous, she thinks, how does the bloghead know what is dangerous? He's been squatting here since he was born in the province and hasn't experienced anything yet. She spits contemptuously.

She has pulled down the zipper of her red overalls and

let the cotton glide over her bare shoulders. She is not wearing a bra. She has casually rolled up the sleeves and legs of the jumpsuit, wearing white Flipp Flopps on her feet.

Wolle comes out.

"You look sloppy," he complains. "Who's going to bite?"

"Let me worry about that," Yna replies. "With me still everyone has bitten.

She looks at wool contemptuously.

"What do you even think you can do to me like that? I am the boss here. Don't forget!

Wolle is angry. He wipes his sweaty hands on his equally red overall, which is full of engine oil stains.

At this moment a white SUV of the VW Touareg brand with a Munich license plate turns into the petrol station. Grazyna is immediately alerted. She arranges her overall, pulls up the zipper and sits the red cap boldly on her blond hair.

"Don't screw it up," Wolle says and quickly withdraws behind the cash register.

Grazyna threatens him inconspicuously and plans to tell him once really clearly that she is the boss of the gas station.

"He probably thinks he can do it with a Polish woman," she mumbles and turns to the customer. The man is middle-aged, wears suit trousers and a white shirt. He has taken off his tie and rolled up his sleeves. Yna looks at him as he approaches.

Aha, he already has white temples, she thinks, and a

small belly base. And his eyebrows are too bushy. I don't like that at all. Strange, that men attach so little importance to it. They really wear their eyebrows right in their faces.

The customer just opens the fuel cap when Yna appears next to the gas pump.

"There's no self-service here," she says friendly with a strong Polish accent. "I'll take care of it."

"Oh, sorry. I didn't know that. Service at the gas station isn't really there anymore."

"Yna puts sex appeal in her voice. "Fill it up?"

"No. The super is extremely expensive here. 20 litres are enough up to Prenzlau."

"We currently have a special offer," says Yna and pulls the zipper of her overalls down to her navel.

Then she takes the nozzle off the hook and inserts it with an erotic back and forth movement into the filler neck of the tank.

"Well, what does that remind you of," she asks, looking at the man provocatively and sharpening her red make-up pout.

"What do you mean?" asks the customer. He seems irritated.

"Well, this one?"

Again, Yna pulls the nozzle out of the tank a few times and reinserts it.

"What's the matter with the offer," asks the customer, who still doesn't understand.

"Well, I am the offer. You'll get me when you fill up."

The man's forehead is sweaty.

"Where?" he asks.

"Well, right here.
"In my car?"
"No, in the staff room."
"And that's free?"
"When you refuel. My mechanic also cleans your windows - while we're busy - and checks the oil level. Well, is that an offer?"

As if by chance, Yna lets the jumpsuit slide over her left shoulder and exposes large parts of her beautiful breast.

"Fill it up," the customer decides.

"Wolle!" Yna shouts. "Continue here. The gentleman and I have something to discuss.

Grazyna takes the man to a steel door next to the toilets. The room behind it is small and stuffy, the window is tilted, but cannot be opened any further because of the row of lockers on the left side of the room. On the right wall there is a simple wooden bench, as found in the changing rooms of sports clubs. A part of it is covered with deck chairs. A further steel door on the rear wall leads to the workshop.

"How do you want me?" Yna asks and pulls off her cap. Her ash blonde hair is short cut and harmonizes beautifully with her deep blue eyes and thick mascara eyelashes.

"Are we going to the bench here?" she asks and makes an inviting movement.

"No, better right here on the wall," says the customer. "Because of the heat.

"Just as you like."

113

Yna now lets her jumpsuit slide all the way down. She doesn't wear any underwear and is therefore ready right away.

"Backwards or forwards," she asks.

"Face the wall," the man says.

Yna stands against the wall with her hands raised, as if she were to be subjected to a body search by the police. And that's how she feels. She hears how the customer opens his trousers and lets them fall down. Then she feels his firm grip on her hip and sees his hairy hands pulling her ass towards him. Shortly thereafter he penetrates her without a word. While he takes her standing, he moans loudly and shows no reserve at all.

"Whore," he pushes out. "You are nothing but a whore!

Yna pulls her face and hopes that the guy will come soon. She thinks about the fact that he at least lets his car fill up. That's exactly what she intended. Finally the man groans and bites her in the neck.

"Ouch, are you crazy," Yna yells at him.

Shocked, the man withdraws from her and quickly pulls up his pants.

"I'm sorry. I forget myself sometimes," he apologizes.

"You can now go to the checkout and pay," Yna says angrily and pushes the man out. Annoyed, she pulls a few paper towels from a dispenser on the wall and rubs herself dry between her legs before pulling up the jumpsuit again.

"Kompletny Idiota," she mumbles, rubbing her sore neck, putting on her cap and leaving the room. She just sees the white SUV quickly turn onto the country road and disappear. Then everything is quiet again. Yna lights a cigarette.

About half an hour later, a red Porsche Carrera 911 GTS Cabriolet, a 140,000 € car with a roaring engine, drives into the petrol station.
"He has probably no problem with the full refueling"; means Wolle. "I guess your trick is not necessary here, boss."
Grazyna sulks.
The young driver of the Porsche jumps out of the car and starts to refuel. Yna watches the fuel gauge. When she stops at 50,- Euro, she curses up.

"Not enough money," Grazyna asks the youngster, sweet as a sugar, as he just closes the fuel cap.
"Too expensive", he replies succinctly.
"Today we have a special offer for full tankers," says Yna and pulls down the zipper. "With you, I don't want to talk around for long. Fill it up once and get a quickie with me as a discount."
"You're kidding me," laughs the handsome boy.
"No, that's completely serious. Well, what do you say to that?
"Sounds interesting," the boy admits. "Are there any other discounts to choose from?"
"Don't you like me?"
"But yes. But I don't like fast sex so much. I like it rather comfortably.
"We can make ourselves comfortable. You put your

car over there at the hedge. It can stand there for a while. Then you get us something to drink from the shop and we go to the back. Well, what do you say? The young man seems to be thinking.

"You want to steal my Porsche as soon as I let it out of my sight. Am I right," he suspects. "Poland is not far from here.

"But no, what do you think. It's just a discount campaign, because nobody fills up anymore. But the business has to run somehow."

"What is your name", the young man wants to know.
"Yna, and you?"

"I am Jens. You're Polish, aren't you?"

"Yes, do you have a problem with that? We Polish women are good at sex. It's common knowledge and I do it without rubber."

"All right. And you do it for free", Jens is still suspicious.

"For the price of a full tank of gas", promises Grazyna.

"So, what is it? Fill up?"
"Agreed."

Shortly afterwards the Porsche parks at the hedge and Grazyna takes Jens into the staff room. Without further ado she slips out of her overall and lies down on the bench.

Jens is not quite on the ball. He listens outside, always afraid to hear the engine of his car. Yna lures him.

"Come on, relax. Nothing happens to your car. I give you my word."

"What does the word of a Polish woman who prostitutes herself matter?" laughs Jens.

"Well, well, what an evil insinuation. My word counts as much as yours. And now come at last".

When Jens finally lies on her and takes her with relish, he relaxes and forgets his car. Yna plays the excited one and actually gives the young man a lot of pleasure. After all, she is not quite inexperienced and has already experienced a lot with regard to sex. Moreover, she likes the boy, even if she envies him for his wealth. Jens moves slowly but surely into Yna's pussy. He doesn't seem to be in a hurry and wants to take as much of this unexpected adventure with him as possible. When he finally reaches his climax, she caresses his hair tenderly.

"Well, did you like it?"

"Great. Can I see you again? I mean, somewhere else where it's nicer and more comfortable. I could pick you up tonight. I pay well too. Certainly better than the gas station attendant."

"Which gas station attendant?" Grazyna asks offended. "Do you mean my mechanic? I am the gas station attendant here.

"You? You own the gas station?"

"What did you think? Do you think I am a Polish whore?"

"No, no. I'm sorry," Jens replies. "Nevertheless. Can you do it tonight?

"Of course not. If you want more, you have to come back for gas. Fill it up, of course.

"Okay. How long are you open?

"See you at eight."

"Maybe I'll be able to empty my tank by then. Then I'll come back."

Jens is enchanted. This Yna is great, he thinks. Better than all the little east girls from the disco. They still live completely behind the moon and know almost nothing.

"So, I must go now", urges Yna and pushes Jens away. "The business is waiting.

A few minutes later she hears the Porsche driving away.

And again these boring hours. The afternoon draws to a close. In the meantime, three women have filled their tanks, all of them only the bare essentials. But Grazyna cannot do anything about women.

"Hire a hustler, boss," suggests Wolle. "Maybe the women are ready to fill up for sex."

Grazyna just grins crookedly.

A small car with a bourgeois in it drives to the gas station.

"Customers", says Wolle.

"Completely useless," Yna replies. "Betting?" Nevertheless, she walks over and plays her game with the nozzle in front of the driver's eyes. She moves it like a penis in traffic. Out and into the filler neck. She drops gasoline, opens her jumpsuit and lets it slide off her shoulder. She even goes so far as to reveal her breasts. But the bourgeois pretends not to understand. He lets Yna fill up with 20 litres and leaves the gas station in a hurry.

118

"I told you so," sulks Yna. "Useless. I know the men very well and I know who is receptive to sex for sale and who is not.

"Interesting! How did you get this knowledge?"

"It's none of your business," Yna replies.

Wolle has become hot from all the talk about sex.

"I think we both go to the staff room now," he says. "I pay too. You need money, don't you?

He reaches for Yna's arm and wants to pull her with him.

"Let go of me," she screams. "You must have gone crazy. Who do you think you are?"

Just at that moment a silver Mercedes SL Roadster comes to the gas station and Jens jumps out.

"Jens, what are you doing here," Yna asks in surprise.

"My old man's car is empty, too. Fill it up, please."

Grazyna gives Wolle a bad look and starts to refuel the Mercedes.

"I really want to sleep with you again," Jens whispers into her ear.

"Your family must be very rich," Yna asks.

"Yes, you can say that. My father got into the tourism business here when nobody else had the idea. He built hotels on the Ucker lakes. Now the industry is booming. The city dwellers seem to love the loneliness here."

"But here at the gas station there is not much tourism to be seen.

"You are simply too far away. People come from the motorway at the Uckermark junction and refuel in

Prenzlau, if at all. I only came here because I like to drive on the lonely streets. That's where I can really turn up. Here we are in the middle of nowhere."

"So true."

Grazyna fills up the Mercedes and takes Jens to the staff room.

"How do you want me this time?" she asks and takes off her clothes.

Jens inhales the smell of petrol and motor oil and feels really at home in this men's domain.

"Better than any perfume," he remarks. "This very special smell of engines, I mean.

"I thought you were here for sex?"

"Yes, I am. But only with you. Please kneel on the bench. I want you from behind."

Yna follows the invitation and squats down. Jens kneels behind her and kisses her buttocks extensively. Then he penetrates her with relish and pushes her wildly and unrestrainedly. Completely different from the first time.

"If my old man knew," he laughs breathlessly. "I'm sure he would have liked to get the discount himself. He's fond of the girls either".

Then he lets himself be carried away by a wave of lust and only comes back to himself when he has satisfied himself.

"My old man has another car," he says when he puts on his trousers. "How long will the discount campaign last? I think I'll send him to you sometime. You should also grant the old people something.

"Yes, send him calmly. The more my action gets

around, the better for business," replies Grazyna.

"So you always want to carry on doing that? Won't that be too much for you?

"No, how so then?

"I mean, you can't sleep with lots of men every day."

"I know what I'm doing," Yna says a little soggy.

What does that boy know about the hardness of life, she thinks. And as it looks, she will never meet him either.

Then she gives in: "Sex is fun for me. For me it's a pleasure and not a burden."

"Then I can pick you up later and we go to my place. I live in a beautiful house at the Unterucker Lake."

Jens does not give up.

"Only here and only with at least 50 litres of super", answers Yna.

Shortly before closing time a potent customer comes again. He drives a BMW X2 SUV in a swanky golden tone. The driver is corpulent and has a bald head. Large stains of sweat spoil his light blue shirt.

Grazyna goes into position and offers himself to the man in a proven way. But he doesn't want to bite. All obscene movements with the fuel gun don't help. He doesn't even respond to the exposure of her breasts.

"Say man," Yna finally asks. "Don't you understand? I offer you sex when you fill up your car."

"I already understood that, girl," answers the man.

"But honestly, it's much too hot for me to have sex. I sweat like a pig even without it".

"I can also give you a blowjob. Then you can sit very

still and don't have to exert yourself. That is also part of the discount campaign. Well, what is it? Oil control and windshield washing included."

"You never let up, do you?"

"Anyway not so fast. Fill it up?"

The man agrees and Wolle takes over the BMW. Yna takes the customer into the staff room, politely asks him to take a seat on the bench and kneels in front of him on a cushion. The man's belly hangs over quite a bit and Yna has trouble opening his pants. Finally she finds his limp penis and begins to raise it by every trick in the book. She whispers obscene words, exposes her breasts and gently massages the penis until it finally stands. Then she bends down and puts it in her mouth. The customer starts moaning and Yna increases the stimulation. Suddenly the man grabs her head with both hands, fixes it and begins to bump into Yna's mouth. He becomes completely ecstatic and moans loudly and beastly. Finally the time has come and he has a violent orgasm. Then he lets go of Yna's head and pushes her away. Yna swallows loudly and gets up.

"It was beautiful, wasn't it?" she asks half-heartedly.

"Not bad," the man answers and closes his trousers.

"But now I have to go. My wife is waiting for me.

At 8 p.m. Grazyna closes the gas station. She is tired and longs for a cool bath. An eventful day lies behind her.

When she opens the gas station the next morning, she doesn't have to wait long for the first customer. A man gets out of an Audi mid-range car and says expectantly to Grazyna, who approaches him bored: "Fill up, please. With a discount".

Yna is not badly surprised.

"Have you been waiting for me to open?"

"Yes, a friend told me about your action and I wanted to be the first. I don't like recently used pussies."

"Wolle," Yna shouts.

"Well, then come with me," she says to the customer. "What's your name?

"Max", is the short answer.

For Yna the man seems to be very unappealing. But business is business, she thinks and takes him to the staff room.

The unappealing man is also quite unbearable during sex and Yna is happy when she finally gets rid of him. She says goodbye to him and waits until she hears the engine of his car before leaving the room. Secretly she has already prepared herself for another boring day with sluggish customers. But everything is different. Word of her discount campaign seems to have got around. One car after the other comes to the petrol station and all the male drivers want to fill up their tanks. This goes so far that Grazyna can no longer leave the staff room. The customers come and go in a continuous stream.

 Between 11 am and the early afternoon Yna doesn't even manage to put on her jumpsuit. She just has time to wipe away one customer's sperm before the next customer claims his discount. Around 5 o'clock she is pretty well done for and closes the gas station without further ado.

She earned well that day, but the price was high. Never before in her life has she experienced anything like it. When she finally lies in her bathtub, she tries to remember all the men she slept with on Sunday. She really can't.

But she doesn't feel bad. Her vagina burns a little, but overall she already had fun. And she has saved her business for now. Of course she wonders how things should continue now. In the long run, of course, she can't keep up with all the sex.

Let's see, she thinks and slurps on her wine glass, maybe this will soon be over again.

The petrol station lies in the dusk as the Polish gas station attendant Grazyna Jablonska watches the scene from the window of her bedroom. She smiles.

The Saint and his Cuddle Bear

Sebastian was 45 years old and still a virgin. Not that
he was ugly, or even marked by God, no, the opposite
was the case. He was quite handsome, tall and slender
with a well cut face under a red-blond head of hair. He
was a bookseller by trade and ran a small antiquarian
bookshop in a medium-sized town in the west. From
his many travels he brought back rare treasures, old
books which he tracked down at flea markets and
brought home like valuable jewellery. He also did not
lack admirers, middle-aged women, who came into his
shop and admired him for having read almost all the
books he offered himself and for being able to
critically reproduce the content. Sebastian was more
often confronted with such women. They winked at
him when they entered his shop or even went so far as
to talk to him about his private life, then he was
embarrassed. He then made some conversation with
them, but quickly pretended to have to make an
important call.

Sebastian's love belonged to God.

He had become religious many years ago. A friend had brought him on the right path with good arguments and a thorough brainwashing. For nights, this friend had sat with Sebastian and read from the Bible. Sebastian, who was at an age when some people are receptive to transcendence, learned that belief in God is the only way not to fall into sinful life in times of sexual freedom and general licentiousness. Only those who remain pure, can hope for a life after this world. His friend belonged to an evangelical fraternity that issued a daily slogan for its followers. He strictly obeyed the instructions, which were as follows: *"I the LORD have called thee in righteousness, and hold thee by the hand," or "Whoso the LORD loves, he rebuke him, and yet he hath pleasure in him as a father in the Son."*

In time Sebastian became more and more lost in faith. He prayed a lot and attended the divine service several times a week. The fact that he was baptized again was only the last consequence of his enlightenment. The denomination to which he now belonged demanded of its members absolute virginity before marriage. At first this seemed to be a heavy burden to the young Sebastian as he was just at the beginning of his manhood and dreamt of trying himself out. But whenever he felt the urge to have sex, he knelt down and prayed to the Lord for help.

And the Lord gave him the strength for chastity. Over time Sebastian got used to having contact with women only on the conversation level. He denied himself physical contact. He grew older and more mature, he did not become more experienced. Had he initially believed that he would soon get married and thus live his sexuality, he gradually withdrew more and more from the women. He knew that his lack of experience made it more and more difficult for him to meet women as he grew older. Nevertheless, he did not give up the desire to marry.

But when he heard other men bragging about their sexual adventures, it dawned on him that he would no longer have the courage to sleep with a woman. He had missed the right time, the moment in youth when a man sleeps with a woman for the first time completely openly and freely, feeling neither fear nor shame, and being as aware of his manly power as a young bull.

Sebastian searched for the tenderness and love that he painfully missed in spite of God's love. He had to take a shower before going to bed and then hold his hands on the blanket. In his sleep he should be pure and belong only to God his Lord.

But Sebastian found a way out.

He bought a plush kangaroo that had looked so cute at him in the toy department of the department store. Nowhere in the Bible was it written that a man was not allowed to have cuddly toys. He sat the stuffed toy on his lap in the evening when he heard his beloved music from Bach. The warmth that the plush animal spread in his loins did him good. And soon he felt that something had become stiff with him, too. Then he pressed the kangaroo stealthily onto the stiff spot and thought of God frightened.

This experience never let him rest. The next evening he put on music again and sat down with his kangaroo on the sofa. And indeed the lust from the evening before came back to him. He paused. Did the Lord want to test him?

But suddenly the lust became so overwhelming that he opened the zipper of his trousers, freed his penis from the sheathing of his underpants and let the kangaroo jump on him, ever more violently and wildly, until he felt relief.

So many of his free evenings passed. The kangaroo, naturally accustomed to jumping, did its service without complaint. His guilty conscience, which at first was a hard burden for him, didn't burden him any more. After all, he touched neither a woman nor himself. What could the Lord object to?

Little by little Sebastian bought more plush animals, which became companions in his secret sexual actions. An elephant, a cat, a piglet and a beautiful round hippopotamus. They were all allowed to jump on him on certain evenings. Sometimes he even went so far as to take one of the animals - the hippopotamus had meanwhile become his favourite - with him to his antiquarian bookshop. Then he moved to the small room in the back. There, hidden between philosophical treatises and Marxist social theories, stood gems of erotic world literature. He enjoyed looking at the books - many of them with illustrations, such as a very old edition of the Kama Sutra. He studied the drawings of positions such as the seesaw, the thigh clamp or the elephant and imagined what this sex with a woman could feel like. Sometimes he would read it until his lust overpowered him and he let his plush animal jump on his penis. He particularly liked the thought that a customer could come to the bookstore at any moment. This increased his ecstasy and he moaned loudly into the loneliness that hung between the dusty books.

Friends and acquaintances who heard about his new passion for cuddly toys - of course without suspecting his sexual background - gave him little cuddly toys for his birthday or Christmas. They now sat everywhere in his apartment and offered a bizarre picture between all the crucifixes, Bible sayings and images of saints.

One day Sebastian strolled along a shopping street in Vienna. He had travelled there to search for antiquarian books because he had heard that there were still treasures to be found in Vienna. Between visits to various flea markets, he wanted to buy a gift for his mother.

Completely unexpectedly, he passed a toy shop with a large light brown teddy bear sitting in its window. Fascinated, Sebastian stopped. The teddy bear was about 1.50 meters high and had a friendly face. Sebastian entered the shop and asked for the price of the bear. It was quite high and it would also be difficult to take the bear home on the plane. He thanked and left the store to continue looking for a gift. But the teddy didn't want to get out of his mind. Back home, he searched the Internet for plush bears and found them. A bear similar to the one from

Vienna looked friendly at him from the monitor. Sebastian thought for a moment, then pressed the shopping cart button and ordered the cute bear.

The bear, or rather the female bear - Sebastian said the animal had a female face - now became his new playmate. He dressed her in women's clothes and gave her the name Irene. From then on Irene slept next to him in his bed and when he suddenly felt like it at night, he simply turned to the side and lay down on his bear. She let everything happen to her and Sebastian didn't have to be afraid to embarrass himself in front of her. So he got to know his own sexuality late, even though he was denied the original encounter with a woman of flesh and blood for the time being.

One day, however, a woman came to his antiquarian bookshop. She had been there several times before, had tried to get Sebastian involved in a conversation and she wouldn't let herself be put off. Sebastian actually liked her. She was perhaps his own age, was slim and had a pretty face with intelligent looking eyes wandering restlessly through the room. She was a musician, which was easy to guess because she almost always had her violin case with her. The woman's clothes were a little strange. She wore pleated skirts with tartan checks and Sebastian had often wondered where she might have bought them. Her blouses were always neatly ironed and she wore them high up. Basically she looked like a governess from a historical film. But she was not uninteresting. She had a strange erotic attraction.

"Hello", she said kindly. "Do you have erotic works of

world literature?"

Sebastian blushed and had to swallow violently. How did this woman know about his secret corner? Had she discovered it by chance and now wanted to test his honesty?

"Yes', he confessed, 'I actually carry a few works. For example one of the oldest erotic works in the world. It is called "Dangerous Liaisons" and was written in the 18th century by Pierre-Ambroise-Francois Choderlos de Laclos. It is a novel of letters".

"Are there any illustrations in this book?" the customer asked

"Yes, there are a few paintings."

The woman wanted to see the book and followed Sebastian into the small room at the back of the crooked shop. Sebastian showed her the few books of this genre and wanted to withdraw discreetly. At that moment the woman gave him a little push, so that he fell on the armchair which he had provided here for his private minutes. Before he knew it, the customer had bent over him and fingered his pants. Very cleverly, she brought out his penis, which was miraculously ready, and sat on it. Then she started riding Sebastian without any warning. He did not know how to defend himself, sent silent prayers to God, but was not heard.

The stranger did her thing well, bouncing and jumping, almost as good as the kangaroo, and in a few minutes she had brought Sebastian to climax. But she didn't seem to have enough. With a single movement she ripped open her impeccable blouse and held her breasts in front of Sebastian's nose.

"Kiss them," she ordered him. "Come on!

Sebastian was so intimidated that he leaned forward
and touched the woman's left breast with his lips.

"More," the woman groaned and Sebastian obeyed.
When the woman felt that he was standing up in her
again, she started her wild ride again. When she finally
let go of Sebastian, he was completely exhausted and
on the verge of a nervous breakdown. But the
customer stood up unmoved, straightened her clothes
and said in a bright voice: "I'll take the book. How
much is it?

Sebastian looked for his glasses, got up and
accompanied the woman to the cash register. She paid
and left the shop with a meaningful smile.

But the Lord did not tolerate the secret happiness of
Sebastian. One day he came back from a journey and
was looking forward to seeing his animal friends again.
When he wanted to unlock his apartment door, he
found it open. He saw signs of burglary and entered
his apartment worried.

What he found there took his breath away. The
burglars had rummaged through all the cupboards and
drawers and had simply thrown many of his beloved
objects onto the floor. But the worst part was that
they had cut open the stomachs of all the cuddly toys.
They probably suspected that the animals were hiding
places for jewellery or money. Irene was the worst
battered. She sat in a corner and the straw hung out of
her body in large flat cakes.

Sebastian dropped to her knees and began to pray.

"Oh Lord, why did you do this to me," he complained. "Why do you want to punish me?"

But then he remembered the 1st commandment. I am the LORD thy God! Thou shalt not have other gods beside me!

Had the LORD blamed him for hanging on to his teddy bear lady? Could he have seen a sub-god in Irene? But that seemed too abstruse to Sebastian. A god who feared the competition of a teddy bear couldn't be too powerful.

And as it was more than 20 years ago, when his friend had missionized him, suddenly a new enlightenment came over Sebastian. He suddenly saw very clearly that he had strayed with his faith into something that lacked any reasonable foundation. Suddenly he began to question. He searched for the sense of chastity that had brought him to the point of satisfying himself with cuddly toys.

Was that really God's will? Was it not rather desirable and natural for man and woman to meet sexually instead of getting lost in a toy world?

Sebastian left his apartment. He drove his car out of the city and out into the country. There he walked for many hours under God's open sky and faced the ghosts of his faith. When he finally returned home completely burnt out, he carefully took the crucifixes and images from the wall and placed them in a cardboard box. He put the "dead" cuddly toys in a garbage bag and brought everything together to the garbage dump.

He was not seen in the community from that day on.

Slowly he recovered from his mental rigidity and returned to normal life. Of course he had a lot to learn and catch up, but in the course of time he became an almost normal man.

And there was one woman who came to his antiquarian bookshop more often than usual. She, too, had changed. She dressed more fashionably and now wore her hair with a modern cut. She had swapped the old-fashioned violin case for a new one, which she was now wearing on her back. She always stayed quite long in Sebastian's shop. And friends claim that they watched Sebastian and the woman leave the store arm in arm.

Two Ladies in Havana

In the bistro on Calle O`Reilly in Havana's old town
the TV was on. It hung over the bar, which was a relic
from the colonial period. It was about ten in the
morning. Ana and Carlota sat at a simple wooden table
and had breakfast. The coffee was good and strong,
but the tortilla they ate almost every morning since
they were in Havana tasted a little bland. Even at this
time of day, a baseball broadcast was on television.
The sound was quite loud and disturbed the two
young Spanish girls in their conversation, so Ana
asked the waiter to turn it down a little.

Ana and Carlota lived in Madrid. There they were
teachers at the same school. During the last school
year they had become friends. Now they used the
summer holidays to recover from everyday stress. Ana
had come up with the idea of flying to Cuba. She
wanted to experience the island in its originality before

the influence of the USA would become too strong.

After breakfast, the two friends strolled a little through La Habana Vieja, the historic old town. They visited an art market and bought some silver earrings and a necklace. Then they walked past the Catedral de la Habana, turned into Calle Empedrado and soon heard live music that seemed to come from a bar.
"Look," Carlota said, "there's the famous Bodeguita del Medio where Ernest Hemingway used to go."
They stopped and let themselves be carried away by the music that came out of the overcrowded bar.
"I would like to drink a Mojito here," Ana remarked.
"Please, do what you can't help. I'll wait for you out here. I don't like the crowds there and rum in the morning isn't my thing anyway".
"Come on, don't be a spoilsport!
But Carlota waved off. So Ana went alone into the Bodeguita, got a bar stool and ordered a Mojito. The band was playing a famous piece of Buena Vista Social Club. Ana felt completely happy and listened to the sound of the flute, which was played expressively by a very beautiful Cuban woman.
The singer of the group, an Afro-Cuban, flirted fiercely with Ana. When the musicians took a break, he came over to her and introduced himself. He asked where beautiful Ana came from and involved her in a conversation about Spain. After a few minutes a group of Americans left the tiny restaurant and Carlota took the chance to check on her friend. She found her laughing and joking with the singer. Typically Ana, she

thought, as soon as you let her out of your sight, she already has a fish on her hook.

Carlota looked around. Everything in the bar was reminiscent of the great writer. Above the bar, behind which a bartender was constantly mixing Mojitos, there was a painting showing Hemingway and next to it photographs of his companions. Quotations from his works were written on the walls, and the guests had immortalized their names for decades. The walls were so densely written on that it was difficult for today's guests to find a place for their names. Even the counter was littered with names.

"Carlota, may I introduce...? Oh, now I've forgotten his name," Ana said.

"What was your name?" she asked the musician.

"Amaury", he laughed. "That is a French name. I am a slave of the Ivory Coast".

"This is my girlfriend Carlota.

Amaury nodded to Carlota.

"Another beautiful one," he said, reaching for his rumba balls lying on the table.

With his colleagues, he lined up to begin the next piece of music. The short break was over.

Ana and Carlota stayed in the bar and listened. The music the group played now had a fast rhythm. One after the other the musicians played solos. Sometimes the player of the double bass stepped out and showed what he could elicit from his instrument, then it was one of the guitarists who showed his skills. But it was the girl on the transverse flute who played best. She stood in all the hustle and bustle and in the heat and produced the most beautiful sounds with her instrument. She seemed as fresh as if she was standing under a tree in the shade.

Amaury conducted a dialogue in a chant with a Cuban man who had just arrived at the bar. He shone all over his face. He also looked fresh, although it was already hot and humid. On the ceiling of the bar two big fans were turning sluggishly.

In the next break Amaury came over to the women and adjusted his giant glasses, which clearly suited socialism, as if he had put them on to confirm the cliché.

"Would you like to go out with me tonight?"

Carlota, who was rather reserved, was about to refuse when Ana happily affirmed.

"Where are you going to lead us," she asked.

"You will see that then. Just come by at 5 pm. Then I have finished here and will be free.

While Ana was looking forward to the evening, Carlota remained skeptical.

"What can happen," Ana asked. "There are two of us. I think it's great that we go out with a local. We will certainly experience something different, something most tourists won't".

On the dot of 5pm the two teachers stood in front of the bar. They had dressed up nicely. Ana wore a short white dress and had put up her full dark hair. Carlota wore her dark curls open and they fell very soft over her shoulders. She wore a strapless shirt with a bell-shaped light mini skirt.

Amaury didn't seem to have expected the women to come. He probably invited women all the time, but seldom succeeded. Anyway, he seemed delighted to see the two Spanish women.

"Okay, let's go," he said obviously in good spirits

No one would have noticed that he had played and sung for at least seven hours. Only his white suit had suffered a little. Amaury took off his jacket, which he had worn bravely all day despite the oppressive sultriness. A black shirt appeared underneath, his sleeves pushed up, releasing his muscular arms. He wore a heavy silver link chain around his neck with a large silver cross hanging from it. A very striking piece of jewellery. Altogether he was a tall lanky guy. He was slim, but not lean, handsome, but not beautiful. His eyes behind the large lenses dominated his dark face. He led Ana and Carlota through the streets of the old town, past the Hotel Plaza and crossed the Passeo de Marti with them. At the corner of Consulado and Neptuno they stopped and waved to one of the private taxis. An old American road cruiser stopped and they climbed onto the worn leather back seat. Amaury said something incomprehensible to the driver and set off through the city's chaotic traffic. Somewhere on La Rampa the taxi stopped and the three got out.

"Over here," Amaury conducted the women.

He led them to a terrace with some plastic tables and chairs. Behind a worn-out counter was a large refrigerator with a glass door, empty except for a few bottles of beer.

Ana was hungry, but found that once again there was only tortilla.

So they ordered tortillas with tomatoes and olives and bought beer.

They had hardly started to eat when a band came into the terrace bar. Amaury jumped up and greeted the musicians with delight.

"The boys will play for us right now," he said. "You will see, they are very good.

And already the first song, "Chan - Chan" by Buena Vista Social Club was played.

Soon Amaury didn't keep it on the chair anymore. He went over to the band, grabbed the microphone and started singing. He fought a kind of duel with the actual singer of the band. But Amaury sang much better and more expressively and the other singer soon gave in. Amaury's appearance changed the music of the group. It became fast and original and fascinated the few guests.

The atmosphere was good and Ana and Carlota were often invited to dance. They danced Cuban salsa as if they were locals, because they had learned to dance in Madrid and often went to salsa bars.

Amaury, who had an eye on Ana, led her to the dance floor again and again. There he danced with her in a very erotic way until he suddenly remembered that he could sing again. Then he just let Ana stand and grabbed the microphone.

Later in the evening, three Russian tourists came with

a beautiful dark-skinned Cuban woman and sat down at a table near the music. The Cuban woman, who was very slim and agile, danced the erotic salsa expressively. She took one man after the other to the dance floor, turned her back to him, moved her hips and swung her little round bottom in front of his abdomen. She made graceful movements with her arms, put them around the man's neck, pulled him down to herself and let him kiss her.

Suddenly two more Cuban women appeared out of nowhere, each taking over one of the men. They also did their job very skilfully, leaving the men a lot of freedom during the dance, being kissed and sometimes touched in piquant places. But when the dance was over, they behaved rather uninvolved. They knew how to eroticize the men so much in the course of the next hour that they could be sure that they could charge any price for their services. And soon Carlota heard that the price for the night was being eagerly discussed at the round plastic table. The Russian men finally agreed to the very high price for Cuban living conditions. Then the three couples set off together, with the men no longer containing themselves and began grabbing and harassing the women on the open street.

Far after midnight the bar closed and Amaury called a taxi to drive back to the old town. After a few minutes it stopped in front of the women's hotel. Amaury paid, squeezed between his companions and put one arm around each waist. Then he set out to go with them to the hotel.

Carlota protested. She had not intended to take the Cuban to the hotel. But Ana took her aside.

"Hey, loosen up," she said to Carlota. "What are you afraid of? We take him up to our room, have a drink and serve him off."

"And you think he'll be so easy to dump?"

"Yes, and if not, then..."

"What then? You don't intend to go to bed with a Cuban stranger, do you?"

"Not necessarily", Ana explained. "But you should take things as they come. I am free and unbound. So why should I renounce a bit of an adventure? And isn't Amaury really a great guy?"

Carlota had to admit that. The Cuban musician was a very extraordinary man. He had a funny way about him that kept making Carlota smile, he was a fantastic musician and certainly a very experienced lover. But the craziest thing about him was his appearance. Amaury underlined his African appearance and his muscular body skilfully through his clothes. His white suit, with the very body-focused pants, accentuated his chocolate brown skin and drew the women's attention to his narrow, plump ass. The shirt with the rolled up sleeves, which he had unbuttoned wide in the meantime, gave a glimpse of his strong arms and his male broad chest. There Carlota saw curly black tufts of hair growing separately, like bushes in the savannah. Carlota had felt the desire all evening to let her hand glide over Amaury's chest. She had no idea whether these tufts of hair were soft or wiry and that made her very curious.

"Well, what now?", Ana urged. "May he accompany us now?

Oh, what can happen, Carlota thought. If he gets pushy, we can put him outside the door. There are two of us.

"Okay, I agree," Carlota finally gave back.

They took the stairs and smuggled Amaury into their room because they knew that Cubans were not allowed to enter a room in a tourist hotel.

In the room, they took beer from the minibar and cheered each other up. Ana turned on the music and immediately started dancing with Amaury. He took off his shirt after a few minutes.

"Too hot," he said and shrugged his shoulders apologetically.

Ana immediately snuggled up to his naked chest and danced with him tightly wrapped through the room.

Carlota sat in the armchair and watched. She had drunk a few beers during the evening and slowly felt the effect of the alcohol. Now she began to envy Ana. She also wanted to dance with Amaury and feel his skin. And she was still irritated by the black curly hair on his chest. Finally she rose and went over to the dancers.

"Hey, let me join in. It's not fair that you dance here alone," she sulked.

Then Ana and Amaury opened their arms benevolently and included Carlota. Now they turned in threes and Carlota noticed in the tumbling round dance the large silver cross hanging down from Amaury's strong neck and swinging back and forth between them. And she felt Amaury's hand gliding down her back and lying on her bottom.

"I'm so hot," Ana moaned suddenly.

She detached herself from Amaury's embrace and pulled the light white summer dress over her head. Dressed only in one thong, she came back to the others.

"And you," Amaury asked. "Aren't you hot?"

While Carlota was still wondering if she should undress, Amaury pulled down her Carmen T-shirt with a quick movement until the smog edge of the neckline slipped under her breasts.

"Muy bonito," Amaury said appreciatively as he saw Carlota's beautiful breasts being pushed up a little by the rubber.

Carlota's skin was naturally light and where her bikini top had protected her from the sun, white round hills with pale pink nipples now stood out from the rest of the sun-brown skin.

Ana laughed in a sillyway and pointed to Carlota: "Ha ha, that looks funny!

Amaury didn't seem to think so, because he bent down to Carlota's breasts and began to kiss them with relish.

"¡Hola!" Ana shouted outraged. "And I! Aren't my breasts beautiful enough for you?

And she wiggled with her full breasts in front of Amauri's eyes. He refused to be asked, released his right hand from Carlota's bottom and put it on Ana's left breast. He seemed to be very skilled in sexual matters because he kept kissing Carlota's breasts and at the same time caressing Ana's breast by paying special attention to her dark nipple.

"Chicas guapas," he muttered and danced skilfully across to the double bed with the two women. Laughing, all three dropped and while Amaury kissed Ana, Carlota took off her shirt and skirt. Then she hesitated for a moment and also took off her delicate lace panties.

Amaury noticed this from the corner of his eye and immediately turned to Carlota. He looked delightedly at her beaver, which was adorned with a narrow stripe of hair. Amaury was apparently a lover of oral sex, for he leaned forward to Carlota, spread her narrow, well-formed thighs and placed his lips on her clitoris. He brought with him particularly favorable conditions for this kind of love play, because his mouth was big and his lips were thrown up and soft.

Another advantage that Africans have over Europeans was what Carlota thought when she felt Amaury's lips and tongue between her legs. But in general the especially large black penis is legendary. She smiled. Ana could apparently read thoughts, because at the same moment she said: "Now let's see if that's true with the big dicks."

She crawled up to Amaury and opened the zipper of his tight pants, which had been suspiciously tight for quite some time. She shoved her hand in, as if she wanted to make sure that there was what she was looking for.

"¡Oh là là!" she exclaimed. "Well, really impressive! And then she took off Amaury's trousers and underpants and freed his troubled penis. Amaury moaned and let Carlota go for a moment when he felt Ana put his penis in his mouth. But then he sucked and sucked on Carlota's pussy.

But Ana finally wanted more. She asked Amaury to lie on his back, got in the riding position and inserted his big penis. Now she began to ride Amaury wildly. who pulled Carlota, who watched disappointedly over to himself.

"Come, squat over my head. Then I can go on," he said friendly.

Carlota did what he had suggested and soon felt his lips and tongue again, which gave her a lot of pleasure. But then she also wanted to enjoy Amaury's penis and asked Ana to change position with her. But Amaury had a better idea.

"Please, both of you lay face down next to each other," he said.

The women obeyed and Amaury entered Carlota from behind, while he worked on Ana's pussy with his fingers. Amaury soon behaved wildly, rode Carlota at a hard fast pace and finally came to a climax.

Now Ana was insulted.

"You were much longer in Carlota than in me. She didn't really want to take you to the room. That is unfair!

"Wait a few minutes," the dark-skinned musician

146

comforted her. "I'll be ready in a minute."

In the time he needed to get excited again, he devoted himself extensively to Anna's beaver. He caressed it with lips and tongue, while Carlota thanked him by teasing him with her lips and tongue.

so it turned out that Amaury was a persistent and imaginative lover. Only towards morning did the three separate from each other and fall asleep contentedly.

The next morning Amaury said goodbye early as his next performance in the Bodeguita del Medio was scheduled for the morning. The two young teachers heard him singing loudly and cheerfully in the shower. They laughed at the thought that he woke up the whole hotel because Amaury had a powerful voice. "And not only that," giggled Ana.

When Amaury had said goodbye, the two women packed their suitcases, for they were about to set off on a tour of Cuba. Amaury had no idea os that. Both they had not mentioned to him that they would leave Havana to never come back.

When their plane took off from Varadero Airport two weeks later, Ana and Carlota looked wistfully out of the small window as they flew over Havana.

"What a pity we didn't meet Amaury again," Ana sighed.

"Better that way," said Carlota. "Something like that never ends well. And we want to stay friends after all".

"Yes, sure. You're right. But Amaury sings so well," Ana answered mischievously.

Laughing, the two teachers leaned back into their seats. They had had a nice stay in Cuba and would tell their friends and colleagues about it. Only one thing should remain their secret, both agreed. No one should ever know about her night with the Afro-Cuban singer.